Lucifer's Harvest

"*Another exciting page-turner by Mel Starr. Confronted by skulduggery in the Black Prince's camp, resolute surgeon Hugh de Singleton risks neck and soul to uncloak the villains. Starr beautifully depicts the sounds, sights and smells, as well as the emotions, of the medieval world in this welcome addition to his long-running series.*"

– Jill Dalladay, author of the *The Abbess of Whitby*

The chronicles of Hugh de Singleton, surgeon

Lucifer's Harvest

The ninth chronicle of
Hugh de Singleton, surgeon

MEL STARR

LION FICTION

Published by Lion Fiction
an imprint of
Lion Hudson plc
Wilkinson House, Jordan Hill Road
Oxford OX2 8DR, England
www.lionhudson.com/fiction

ISBN 978 1 78264 188 9
e-ISBN 978 1 78264 189 6

First edition 2016

A catalogue record for this book is available from the British
Library

Printed and bound in the UK, October 2016, LH26

For Nick, Alex, Elliot, and Oliver

"A day of battle is a day of harvest for the devil"
Rev. William Hook; 1600–1677

Acknowledgments

Several years ago, when Dan Runyon, Professor of English at Spring Arbor University, learned that I had written an as yet unpublished medieval mystery, he invited me to speak to his fiction-writing class about the trials of a rookie writer seeking a publisher. He sent sample chapters of Master Hugh's first chronicle, *The Unquiet Bones*, to his friend Tony Collins. Thanks, Dan.

Thanks to Tony Collins and all those at Lion Hudson who saw Master Hugh's potential. Thanks especially to my editor, Jan Greenough, who, after nine books, knows Master Hugh as well as I do, and excels at asking such questions as, "Do you really want to say it that way?" and, "Wouldn't Master Hugh do it like this?"

Dr. John Blair, of Queen's College, Oxford, has written several papers about Bampton history. These have been invaluable in creating an accurate time and place for Master Hugh. Tony and Lis Page have also been a great source of information about Bampton. I owe them much. Tony died in March 2015, only a few months after being diagnosed with cancer. He will be greatly missed.

Ms. Malgorzata Deron, of Poznan, Poland, offered to update and maintain my website. She has done an excellent job. To see the result of her work, visit www.melstarr.net

Glossary

Aketon: a padded coat, worn beneath armor to absorb blows, or on its own by ordinary soldiers.

Aloes of lamb: lamb sliced thin and rolled in a mixture of egg yolk, suet, onion, and various spices, then baked.

Ambler: an easy-riding horse, because it moved both right legs together, then both left legs.

Angelus Bell: rung three times each day – dawn, noon, and dusk. Announced the time for the Angelus devotional.

Assumption Day: August 15. Celebrated the assumption to heaven of Mary, the mother of Christ.

Bailiff: a lord's chief manorial representative. He oversaw all operations, collected rents and fines, and enforced labor service. Not a popular fellow.

Bolt: a short, heavy, blunt arrow shot from a crossbow.

Braes: medieval underpants.

Burgher: a town merchant or tradesman.

Captal de Buch: an archaic feudal title. In 1370 the holder was Jean de Grailly, praised as an ideal of chivalry.

Chapman: a merchant, particularly one who traveled from village to village with his wares.

Chauces: tight-fitting trousers, often of different colors for each leg.

Chrismatory: a container for holy oil.

Cinq Ports: five ports on the English Channel, closest to France: Hastings, Hyth, Dover, Sandwich, and New Romney. (Mayor of New Romney in the 1590s was Thomas Starr.)

Coppice: to cut back a tree so that a thicket of saplings would grow from the stump. These shoots were used for everything from arrows to rafters, depending upon how long they were allowed to grow.

Cotehardie: the primary medieval garment. Women's were floor-length, while men's ranged from thigh- to ankle-length.

Crenel: open space between the merlons of a battlement.

Cresset: a bowl of oil with a floating wick used for lighting.

Cuisse: plate armor defense for the thigh.

Daub: a clay and plaster mix, reinforced with straw or horse hair.

Dexter: a war horse, larger than pack horses, palfreys, and runcies. Also, the right hand direction.

Easter Sepulcher: a niche in the wall of a church or chapel where the host and a cross were placed on Good Friday and removed on Easter Sunday.

Egg leach: a thick custard, often enriched with almonds, spices, and flour.

Fast day: Wednesday, Friday, and Saturday. Not the fasting of modern usage, when no food is consumed, but days upon which no meat, eggs, or animal products were consumed. Fish was on the menu for those who could afford it.

Free company: at times of peace during the Hundred Years' War bands of unemployed knights would organize themselves and ravage the countryside. France especially suffered.

Gathering: eight leaves of parchment, made by folding the prepared hide three times.

Gentleman: a nobleman. The term had nothing to do with character or behavior.

Halberd: a long pole with axe blade attached, and topped with a spike.

Harbinger: a scout sent ahead of the army to find lodging.

Hind: female of the red deer.

Kirtle: a medieval undershirt.

Lammastide: August 1, when thanks was given for a successful wheat harvest.

Liripipe: a fashionably long tail attached to a man's cap.

Lych gate: a roofed gate through the churchyard wall under which the deceased rested during the initial part of a funeral.

Mangonel: a siege engine used to throw missles to break down a city wall.

Marshalsea: the stables and assorted accoutrements.

Maslin: bread made from a mixture of grains, commonly wheat or barley and rye.

Merlon: a solid portion of a castle wall between the open crenels of a battlement.

Michaelmas: September 29. The feast signaled the end of the harvest. Last rents and tithes were due.

Nine man morris: a board game similar to tic-tac-toe, but much more complicated.

Ninth hour: about 3 pm.

Palfrey: a riding horse with a comfortable gait.

Poleaxe: also called a halberd.

Pomme dorryse: meatballs made of ground pork, eggs, currants, flour, and spices.

Porringer: a small round bowl.

Portcullis: a grating of iron or wood hung over a passage and lowered between grooves to prevent access.

Pottage: anything cooked in one pot, from soups and stews to a simple porridge.

Reeve: an important manor official, although he did not outrank the bailiff. Elected by tenants from among themselves, often the best husbandman. He had responsibility for fields, buildings, and enforcing labor service.

Remove: a course at dinner.

Runcie: a common horse of lower grade than a palfrey or ambler.

St. Bartholomew's Day: August 24.

St. John's Day: June 24.

St. Thomas the Apostle's Day: July 3.

Shingle: a stony, heavily graveled beach.

Solar: a small private room, more easily heated than the great hall, where lords often preferred to spend time, especially in winter. Usually on an upper floor of a castle or great house.

Sole in cyve: sole boiled, then served with a sauce of white wine, onions, bread crumbs, and spices.

Squire: a youth who attends a knight, often in training to become knighted.

Stockfish: inexpensive fish, usually dried cod or haddock, consumed on fast days.

Stone: fourteen pounds.

Trebuchet: a medieval military machine which could hurl stones with great force – similar to a mangonel.

Tun: a large cask capable of holding over 200 gallons.

Victualer: responsible for finding food for an army on the move.

Villein: a non-free peasant. He could not leave his land or service to his lord, or sell animals without permission. But if he could escape his manor for a year and a day he would be free.

Wattle: interlacing sticks used as a foundation and support for daub in forming the walls of a house.

Whitsuntide: Pentecost, seven weeks after Easter Sunday: "White Sunday".

Wimple: a cloth covering worn over the head and around the neck.

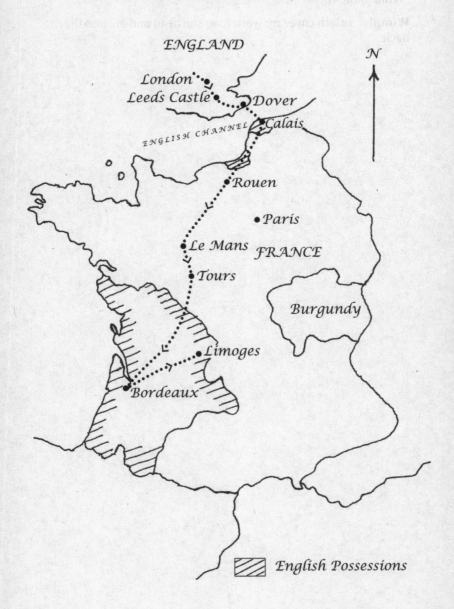

Chapter 1

When I first traveled to France I did not rue the journey. I was a student, and like most lads eager to see new lands and learn new things. I was then on my way to Paris to study surgery at the university.

I was less eager to cross the sea in the year of our Lord 1370 when Lord Gilbert Talbot, my employer, required it of me. France was no longer a new land to me, and perhaps I had lost the desire to learn new things. I learned many new things anyway. Knowledge is not always desired or intended. It is, however, often useful, even if unwanted, and accumulates like the grey whiskers which Kate occasionally finds in my beard. At least for this journey I would ride a palfrey rather than walk.

Three days before Whitsuntide I awoke to a pounding upon Galen House door. My Kate was already from our bed and called out that Arthur must speak to me. Arthur is a groom to Lord Gilbert Talbot and has been useful to me and his employer in helping untangle several mysteries which fell to me to solve. The fellow is made like a wine cask set upon two coppiced stumps, with arms as thick through as my calves.

I am Hugh de Singleton, surgeon, and bailiff to Lord Gilbert Talbot at his manor of Bampton. I assumed that Arthur's early appearance at my door meant that someone in the castle required my surgical skills.

This was so, but not in the manner I expected.

I drew on chauces, donned my cotehardie, ran my fingers through my hair, and descended the stairs. Arthur stood dripping upon the flags at the entrance to Galen House. The day had dawned grey and wet. Arthur would not, I thought, be about in such weather unless propelled by some important matter.

"I give you good day," he said, and continued before I could ask his business. "Lord Gilbert wishes speech with you this

15

morning. 'Tis a matter of import, he said, and asks for you to wait upon him without delay."

"Is m'lord ill, or injured? Or some other in the castle? Shall I take instruments and herbs?"

"Nay. Lord Gilbert's well enough, an' all others, so far as I know. Didn't tell me why he wished words with you; just said I was to seek you an' give you his message."

"Which you have done. Return to the castle and tell Lord Gilbert I will be there anon."

I splashed water upon my face to drive Morpheus from me, hastily consumed half of a maslin loaf, and swallowed a cup of ale. Weighty matters should not be addressed upon an empty stomach. Half an hour later I walked under the Bampton Castle gatehouse, bid Wilfred the porter "Good day," and set my path toward the solar where I expected to find Lord Gilbert.

But not so. John Chamberlain was there, and told me that my employer was at the marshalsea. I descended the stairs to the yard, crossed to the stables, and found Lord Gilbert in conversation with Robert Marshall and a gentleman I had not before seen.

"Ah, Hugh, you have come," Lord Gilbert greeted me. "I give you good day. Here is Sir Martyn Luttrel with news from France. Hugh, Sir Martyn, come with me. We will speak in the solar."

News from France which must be discussed in the solar could not be agreeable. I had no hint of Lord Gilbert's topic, but assumed the conversation would have something to do with the burly stranger who had appeared at Bampton Castle. So it did.

When we were seated Lord Gilbert explained his reason for calling me to him.

"Sir Martyn has brought disquieting news from France," he began.

'Twas as I feared. News from France is often troubling. Much like news from Scotland.

"King Charles has announced that he is confiscating Aquitaine, in violation of the Treaty of Bretigny. No matter how many times we vanquish the French they will not remain subdued. The Duke of Berry has even now an army approaching Aquitaine.

"Prince Edward has sent for knights and men-at-arms from England to assist him in opposing the French king. I am his liegeman, and am required to provide five knights, twelve squires, and twenty archers and men-at-arms. My chaplain will accompany us, and I wish to have a surgeon as a member of my party."

So far as I knew Lord Gilbert had but one surgeon in his employ; me.

I was speechless at this announcement. Lord Gilbert saw my mouth drop open and continued before I could voice objections which were forming in my mind.

"You have crossed to France once already," he said, "so know that the passage is not arduous in summer."

When we might return no man could know. Returning to England in December did not bear thinking about.

"And I am not so young as I once was," he continued. "I am yet fit for battle, but 'twould be well to have you at hand should some French knight strike a lucky blow. Or unlucky, depending upon one's loyalties," he laughed.

"But what of folk here?" I finally stammered. "If I travel with you to France there will be no bailiff to see to the manor. Who will serve in my place to collect rents at Michaelmas?"

"John Prudhomme has served well as reeve. I intend to appoint him to your post till we return. Your Kate I would have oversee the castle," he continued. "'Tis not a duty beyond a woman. Lady Petronilla did so when I was at Poitiers and she was then younger than Kate. I have no one to leave in charge of Richard but his nurse, and 'tis not meet for a woman of such station to supervise a castle. John Chamberlain will deal with most matters. Kate will not be much troubled."

I knew what Kate's opinion of this move would be, but before I could explain my wife's loyalty to Galen House Lord Gilbert continued:

"Kate will lodge in Lady Petronilla's chamber. It has been

17

empty since the Lord Christ took her from me, but I will see that it receives a good cleaning. 'Tis a large chamber. Plenty of room for Bessie and Sybil."

Lord Gilbert had considered that I might object and answered my protests before I could voice them.

But for one matter.

"Warfare is a perilous business," I said. "What if I am slain in battle or captured and held for ransom? Who will care for my family? I am not wealthy. Kate would find few resources if I was taken and held for ransom."

This assumed that a French knight would believe a poor surgeon's life worth the trouble of sparing for a trifling ransom.

"Oh," Lord Gilbert said, pulling at his beard. "Just so. I pay your wages, so have some thought as to your value. What say you, Hugh? What are you worth?"

"To you, or to Kate and Bessie and Sybil?"

"A fair question. Would one hundred pounds serve for ransom if you are taken, and ten pounds each year to Kate if, the Lord Christ forbid, you are slain? Neither is likely, mind you. 'Tis my thought that, if this expedition comes to a battle, you will be far from the field, prepared with your instruments and physics to deal with wounds."

"What if you also are slain?" I said. "Or seized? Who then will provide for Kate?"

"I will see an Oxford lawyer and have drawn up a document which will serve as your security in this matter. Does that satisfy you?"

The tone of his voice told me that Lord Gilbert was becoming exasperated with my objections. I decided that I must make no further protest. If a great lord wishes a man to accompany him to France it is best for the fellow to see the journey as an opportunity rather than an obligation and make the best of it. Priests often assign travel as a penance, and with good reason, but after all, France is not Scotland.

Sir Martyn was present for this conversation but took no part in it other than to turn his head from me to Lord Gilbert as we spoke in turn. Lord Gilbert's conversation now turned to his visitor.

"Where are you bound this day?" he asked.

"I am to seek Sir John Trillowe, then Sir Richard Coke and Sir Ralph Lull on the morrow."

"How many knights and men-at-arms has the prince called for?" I asked.

"Three hundred knights are bid come to France," Sir Martyn replied. "With a thousand squires, pages, archers, and men-at-arms."

"We are to assemble at Dover on St. Thomas the Martyr's Day," Lord Gilbert added, speaking to me. "Where ships are even now being assembled to carry us to Calais."

"This being so," Sir Martyn said, "I must be away to complete my task. You and the others have but a month to prepare and make your way to Dover. I came first to you."

"Stay for dinner," Lord Gilbert said. "You can easily travel to East Hanney this afternoon to inform Sir John of Prince Edward's command."

Throughout the realm other messengers were informing knights and their men of this requirement for their services. Many, perhaps most, would welcome the summons. Peace can be boring and war may be profitable – if a rich castle can be plundered or a wealthy French knight captured and held for ransom.

Lord Gilbert invited me to stay for dinner that day at the castle. The meal was of five removes, regardless of the king's requirement that two removes be the limit. If Edward should learn of Lord Gilbert's violation I suspect he will permit the transgression to pass.

The announcement of my forthcoming journey did not harm my appetite. Very little does. I stuffed myself with parsley bread and honeyed butter, fruit-and-salmon pie, sole in cyve, aloes of lamb, and pomme dorryse. So when I departed the castle I was well sated. Kate knows that upon occasions when I am called to the castle my return to Galen House is uncertain, so had fed herself and our daughters rather than await my return.

Rain had continued, so I shook my cotehardie free of such water as possible, stamped mud from my shoes, and thereby soiled Kate's clean floor. Here was no way to begin an account of the morning's tidings which would likely trouble my spouse. But I thought of this too late. 'Tis impossible to unstamp a foot and replace mud upon a shoe.

"What news, husband?" Kate said from the kitchen, then appeared in the doorway. She looked from my sodden cap to the muddied flags and frowned. My announcement did not improve her expression.

"Lord Gilbert is called to France," I began, "and bids me accompany him. He will have you occupy a chamber in the castle to oversee his son and the lad's nurse."

"And leave Galen House? What of Bessie and Sybil?"

"You and they will have Lady Petronilla's chamber in the castle. It has remained empty since she died. Lord Gilbert promised to have it put right before you move to the castle. The walls of Lady Petronilla's chamber are hung with many fine tapestries," I added by way of persuasion.

"When? How long till this is to happen?"

"Not long. A week perhaps. We are to be in Dover to take ship for France by St. Thomas the Martyr's Day. I think Lord Gilbert will require at least a fortnight for the journey to Dover, or near so."

Next morn I was busy with my instruments, sharpening blades with an oiled stone I keep for the purpose, when Arthur again thumped my door with his meaty fist.

"Lord Gilbert says we will leave Bampton Tuesday morn," he said. "I am to help you move Mistress Kate to the castle. I'll bring a cart an' runcie Monday at the ninth hour, that bein' acceptable."

"The ninth hour will serve. We will make ready."

We did. Kate packed our largest chest with clothing for herself and our daughters, and I filled a smaller chest with my own garments, and bags of crushed hemp and lettuce seeds, and betony. I also placed a jar of St. John's Wort ointment in the chest, for I was likely to see wounds aplenty before I returned to Bampton. My instruments chest I keep ready for use so nothing of preparation was necessary but for the sharpening of blades.

On Sunday, after mass, as this was to be our last meal together in Galen House for many months, Kate used her supply of eggs to prepare an egg leech for our dinner. That night, after dark, when the fowl would be roosting, I intended to send pages from the castle to collect Kate's hens and cockerel from the coop and add them to the castle poultry, till those of us off to restore King Edward's privileges could return.

Arthur was prompt, and we soon had the cart loaded. I lifted Kate and Bessie and Sybil to the cart, watched as Arthur led the runcie down Church View Street, then turned to Galen House to affix a lock to the door. The rear door I had already barred from within.

This was the second house on the site to bear the name of the great physician of antiquity. My first house, a gift from Lord Gilbert, had been burned to ashes by Sir Simon Trillowe, he being furious that I, a slender surgeon with an equally slender purse and a large nose, had won Kate Caxton for my bride. His father had been, at the time, sheriff of Oxford, and he a handsome young knight who had little experience of failure or denial. When Kate chose my suit over his he was enraged. Fortunately a new sheriff took office, a friend to Lord Gilbert, and when 'twas proven that Sir Simon set my house ablaze he required of the knight ten pounds to rebuild Galen House.

Last week Sir Martyn was to call Sir John, Sir Simon's father, to join the force summoned to aid Prince Edward in France. The son would surely accompany his father on this expedition.

Sir Simon was no longer so handsome as he had once been. His left ear protruded from the side of his skull in a most unbecoming fashion. A brawl upon the streets of Oxford had left the fellow battered and bleeding and with an ear hanging from his head by but a wisp of flesh. I was in Oxford and nearby at the time and was summoned to stitch the dangling ear back to Sir

Simon's bruised skull. I did so, but such a repair is difficult, an ear being all gristle and nearly impenetrable by even the sharpest needle. And I had no experience at such a reconstruction.

Sir Simon did not lose his ear. My surgery was successful, mostly. When the injured appendage healed it extended from the side of his head. For this asymmetry he blamed me, not understanding how difficult it is to remodel an ear, nor realizing that without my effort he might now have no ear at all. Ungrateful wretch.

To this disfigurement add his choler at losing Kate to me, and his arson is understandable, if wrongheaded.

As I followed the cart down Church View Street to Bridge Street I resolved that for the next few months I would avoid turning my back to Sir Simon Trillowe. As it happened, 'twas Sir Simon who should not have turned his back to another.

Chapter 2

Kate busied herself making Lady Petronilla's chamber into a home for herself and our daughters whilst I stayed mostly out of her way. I was pleased that leaving Galen House to become temporary mistress of Bampton Castle did not displease Kate so much as I had thought it might. 'Twas not the first time I had mistaken her sentiments and surely would not be the last, I thought, unless I found a grave in France. Death ends all errors, then comes time to repent of them. I am a man, and like other males am often mistaken when attempting to predict female opinions.

Supper that evening at Bampton Castle was more elaborate than usual, at Lord Gilbert's request, it being his last meal in the castle hall for many months. Perhaps, as we were about to set off to do battle, it might be his last meal in the castle forever. This, however, was a thought no man wished to voice, and so jesting and jollity reigned, with many remarks between removes of the unamiable things we would do to the French king and his knights.

I could not drive from my mind that night, as I took to my bed, that this might also be the last I would see of Kate. Life is tenuous, even for her who would remain in England, safe behind castle walls. More so for me, who was about to cross the sea, eat unpalatable food, live in noisome conditions, and eventually be cast among armed men who wished me ill.

I awoke well before the Angelus Bell, which Lord Gilbert had said would be the signal for all to assemble in the castle yard. I believe most others of our cohort spent as sleepless a night as I, for men were assembled between hall and portcullis while it was yet too dark to recognize a face from more than two or three paces away. Until John Chamberlain lit a torch.

Lord Gilbert's cook laid out fresh wheaten loaves, cheese, and ale with which we who would travel this day, and those who remained, might break our fast. Agnes, Arthur's wife, clung close to him, their infant in her arms. She had lost one husband and feared, I think, the loss of another. Perhaps Kate also dreaded the future, but she did not speak of her concern. Nor did I. "Sufficient to the day is its own evil," I had read a few weeks past in my Bible. This seemed an appropriate time to obey the injunction to cease worry about days to come.

So between bites of bread and cheese we spoke of my return, and plans for the future, when we would again together shelter under the roof of Galen House.

"Take care, husband," Kate finally said, "and return to me hale and whole."

"I intend to stay far away from French swords and arrows," I said. "I have accumulated enough scars in Lord Gilbert's service."

Kate ran her fingers across the pale line crossing my forehead and cheek. This track was the result of being beaten and kicked a year past when men took amiss my investigation into bones found in the St. John's Day fire in Bampton. And beneath my kirtle and cotehardie was the healed wound where an arrow had pierced my side whilst I searched for the felon who had slain a chapman near to St. Andrew's Chapel, to the east of Bampton. As I thought of the wound it began to itch. If the future is measured by the past, my return to Kate unmarred seemed dubious. This I did not say.

Bampton Castle yard was crowded with men and women saying their farewells. Eight carts and the runcies to draw them, laden with armor, swords, bows, arrows, and oats for our beasts and food for men, also clogged the enclosure. In addition there were palfreys and amblers and, led by mounted pages, seven dexters for combat should this expedition come to blows with a French force.

I had no responsibility for this host but to accompany it, but this nearly changed before we passed under the castle portcullis. One of the dexters became offended by a page who perhaps yanked too energetically upon the stallion's lead. The beast signaled his displeasure by lashing out with his forefeet, one of which caught the lad in the ribs and sent him sprawling to the cobbles.

I dismounted and hastened to the youth, who was red-faced with embarrassment. Fortunately that was the extent of his injury. I prodded his ribs, which were tender and would no doubt be purpled before the day was out, but discovered no broken bones. The page regained his feet, took the dexter's reins from another who had secured the agitated beast, and this time gently led the animal to his own palfrey. I saw the page grimace as he climbed to his saddle.

A farewell kiss for Kate, Bessie, and Sybil, thence to the palfrey's saddle, and I was off for France. I caught one last glimpse of Kate, waving farewell, as my beast clattered across the castle drawbridge. My mood became somber and I could not help but consider when, if ever, I would again see my family. Perhaps others of the company felt the same, for I noticed that men who moments before had been jesting and shouting farewell fell silent as we passed from the castle forecourt to Mill Street.

Horses and men were fresh and carts were new, so we reached Oxford before the ninth hour. Lord Gilbert and his knights were provided chambers in the castle, whilst we lesser mortals made do with tents in the castle yard.

Shortly after my tent was erected I heard a man call my name. 'Twas a groom in service to the sheriff of Oxford who sought me. He told me that Lord Gilbert wished me to wait upon him in the sheriff's chamber.

I found my employer with Sir Thomas de la Mere, newly appointed Oxford's sheriff, and his clerk. The clerk had before him two documents and I soon discovered what they were. Lord Gilbert had not forgotten his promise to me. He had dictated to the clerk the terms he had pledged if I was taken and held for ransom or slain. Lord Gilbert had signed the documents, and Sir Thomas also, as witness.

"Sir Thomas will keep one of these parchments here, at the castle," Lord Gilbert said. "You may have the other, to safeguard as you wish."

A few streets from the castle is the stationer's shop where my father-in-law, Robert Caxton, does business with Oxford scholars. I had intended to call upon him this day and had now another reason to do so. It seemed to me foolish to take Lord Gilbert's pledge with me to France. Was I to perish there, who would know of its terms?

Oxford's streets were clogged. Fuzzy-cheeked lads in new gowns laughed and pushed one another as they enjoyed the life of carefree scholars. I remembered when I was such a one.

My father-in-law had injured himself some years past, falling from a ladder, and I had removed a splinter from his back which had caused a festering sore. For this service he had promised me as many gatherings of parchment as I might need, and pots of ink as well. He was also influenced to look favorably upon me when, a few months later, I asked his permission to pay court to his beautiful daughter.

I had not seen Robert Caxton for more than a year. I was surprised at his appearance. His hair had become wispy and white, and he walked bent from the waist, as if it pained him to stand erect.

But there was joy in his face when I told him of Kate and Bessie and Sybil. I saw also longing in his eyes, but thought it unlikely that he would ever again see his daughter in this life. He was become too frail to walk to Bampton, and with two children to care for Kate could not readily come to him. Perhaps, if I returned from France in good time, I might commandeer a cart from the castle marshalsea and bring my family to Oxford.

I produced Lord Gilbert's pledge and explained the need for the document. Caxton nodded understanding and promised to keep the sheet of parchment in his chest. I also asked of him a pot of ink and two gatherings of parchment. I thought it likely that there might be events in France in weeks to come worthy of recording. So there were.

Next morning we were off for London. We halted for the night at Watlington and before dark Sir John Trillowe, and his knights, squires, pages, and men-at-arms joined our camp.

Among his knights I saw Sir Simon. The knight wore his cap and liripipe in such a fashion that it obscured his protruding ear. I saw two pages who wore their liripipes coiled the same. Sir Simon had unwittingly become an influence of style.

We reached London the evening of the third day after departing Oxford. Other of the knights called to France had arrived before us. The city was brimming with swaggering men bragging to all who would listen – especially pretty maids – of what was to befall the French should they contest the restoration of King Edward's possessions and rights.

We raised our tents in a field near to the abbey of Westminster. Not all of us. Lord Gilbert was a guest of the abbey. King Edward is unwell, although his ailment is not such that a surgeon could deal with it. Nor physicians, either, if tales be true. 'Tis said that the king has grown remote since Queen Philippa died last year, although 'tis also said that he does not lack for female companionship.

Lord Gilbert and the other great barons of the realm who were bound for France would not pass through London without calling upon the king, so the field where we camped became a morass for the tramping of feet and hooves while we more humble folk waited for the audiences to be done. The second day after arriving at Westminster, after mass in the abbey church, we broke camp and set out for London Bridge and Kent.

Two days later we stopped to rest at Leeds Castle. I believe till then Sir Simon had not known of my presence in Lord Gilbert's cohort. But that evening, just before dark, I met him and another coming about a tent which lay between my own shelter and a well.

The knight did not at first recognize me, I think. The light was failing and his eyes were down, watching for ruts in the path which might trip a man. The field where the tents had been erected was already becoming a muddy bog after but a few hours.

Sir Simon raised his eyes to see who approached, and I saw recognition and then hatred flash across his face. I expected such a glare from the fellow, but did not expect what came next.

Our paths were such that we would pass but an arm's length from each other. I was prepared to recognize Sir Simon with a nod of my head and to wish him "Good eve," but as I was about to do so he turned toward me and in the dim light I caught a glimpse of his right fist appearing on a path toward my chin. The man had nursed a grudge for three years. For the next week I nursed a tender lip.

Sir Simon had not had time to cock his fist for a telling blow, I think. 'Twas a spur-of-the-moment act, so the stroke was not so forceful as might have been. I saw his fist coming and was able to turn away, so did not receive the full force of Sir Simon's attack. This was a good thing. Sir Simon was not a small man.

But together my twisting to evade the blow and Sir Simon's fist against my chin caused me to stumble and lose my balance. I fell heavily into the side of a tent, which then collapsed under me. My weight then pulled stakes from the soft soil from the opposite side of the tent and the entire fabric fell in upon itself.

The tent was not empty. My prostrate form fell across a man who had taken to his pallet for the night. The fellow was startled from sleep, found himself enmeshed in the folds of his fallen tent, and roared his displeasure. I was soon snarled in the tent, its ropes, and the struggle of the man beneath me. I heard Sir Simon and his companion laugh.

I managed to free myself soon enough to see Sir Simon making off, no doubt pleased with himself. Half the camp surely heard the cursing and struggle coming from the toppled tent. A man unknown to me hurried to the place and helped me untangle myself from ropes and canvas, then together we freed the hapless fellow I had so rudely awakened.

"What had Sir Simon against you?" my helper asked when we had drawn the sleeper from his canvas prison.

"You saw?" I said whilst gently rubbing my tender lip.

"Aye. Not difficult to cross Sir Simon. Done so myself."

"'Tis a long story," I replied.

"Keep your guard up," the fellow said. "Sir Simon is rarely satisfied with one blow."

"I am Hugh de Singleton," I said. "Surgeon to Lord Gilbert Talbot. Who was the fellow with Sir Simon?"

"A surgeon? Good man to know, if worst comes to worst. I am Sir John Clifford. But I pray we need not meet again," he chuckled. "Sir Simon's companion was John de Boys. Like Castor an' Pollux, those two."

The inhabitant of the tent, meanwhile, had found his cotehardie in its ruins. He spoke as Sir John turned to continue upon his way.

"Was it you who fell upon my tent? If you must drink overmuch wine so you cannot stand aright, do so nearby your own tent," the man growled. He advanced toward me and I feared that I was to receive another blow.

"Nay," I protested. "I've had no wine. A man assaulted me just now and I fell against your tent. Here, I will help you erect it again."

"I heard you say that you are Lord Gilbert's surgeon. Why would some man attack a surgeon?"

"Because," I replied, "I made a weathervane of his ear."

The fellow peered at me with a puzzled expression but asked no more of the altercation. Together we re-erected the tent and I continued to my own tent, which I shared with Arthur and Uctred.

There is little to do in such an encampment but sit about a fire, drink too much ale, throw dice, and tell stories of past exploits. Under the influence of blaze and ale these tales grow marvelously. I found Arthur with the others of Lord Gilbert's cohort, sitting placidly whilst a page barely old enough to produce threadlike whiskers concluded a report of his conflict with a cutpurse on the streets of Oxford.

"What was the uproar about?" Arthur asked. "'Eard a row a few minutes past. You see it?"

"Aye... saw it clearly."

I fell silent and sat upon the end of Arthur's bench. When I said no more, he said, "Well?"

"Met Sir Simon," I said through a thickening lip.

"'Twas a noisy encounter. We heard it. What happened?"

I told him, and when I was done Arthur leaned close and peered at my lip in the firelight.

"Swole up already," he said. "Gonna dribble your ale into your beard for a few days. Next I see Sir Simon, be he alone, or with but one or two others, I'll 'ave words with 'im 'bout the folly of attacking Lord Gilbert's surgeon."

I had no doubt that, if such a conversation occurred, 'twould be one-sided.

Chapter 3

We set out next morn for Canterbury and two days later pitched our tents beside the town wall. Many sought the cathedral and knelt at the tomb of Thomas Becket in the crypt to ask the saint's blessing in the travel and combat to come. Whether or not the archbishop heard from heaven and looked favorably upon these requests I know not. It seems to me that the saint, if he harkened to such pleas, would take them then to the Lord Christ. Why, then, not address such petitions directly to Him?

Such thoughts are perhaps heretical, and so I keep them to myself. A few years past I spoke my mind about purgatory to a dying abbot and nearly ran afoul of an archdeacon when my words were overheard. A man seldom gets in trouble for saying too little.

After a day of rest for men and beasts we set out for Dover and reached the port on the evening of the second day from Canterbury. Lord Gilbert and others of rank made their abode in the castle whilst all others pitched tents at the base of the hill where the castle overlooks town and sea. We were told to be ready to strike our tents and assemble at the harbor at a moment's notice. The port was overflowing with vessels of all sizes, accumulated from the Cinque Ports and even farther away. We waited for two days for the wind to veer from the west.

A man possessing the lungs of a bellowing bull came through the camp before dawn two days before St. Thomas the Martyr's Day, charging all to be at the ships by the third hour.

I had not seen Lord Gilbert since our party arrived at the walls of Canterbury. He glanced in my direction at the wharf where our ship was tied, then turned to study me more thoroughly. My lip was yet red, swollen, and tender to the touch. He would likely ask of the cause at some convenient time.

Lord Gilbert's rank meant that he and his men could board ship from the wharf. Others of lesser position crossed the shingle and waded to their vessels in waist-deep water. 'Twas July, and the sea near as warm as would ever be, but I was pleased not to be required to embark in such a fashion. Rank has its privileges, even for those who but serve a man of rank.

By the sixth hour most of our fleet was well off shore. To the east and west I saw the white cliffs gleaming and thought how welcome that sight would be upon our return.

The wind was brisk. This was both good and bad. We would reach Calais the sooner, but the farther we traveled from land the stronger the breeze became, till 'twas nearly a gale. This raised considerable waves and soon *mal de mer* began to afflict those of us accustomed to a steady floor beneath our feet.

"Feels like I've 'ad too much wine," Arthur said, and plunged to the bulwark. Uctred and several others had preceded him to the rail, and more would follow. The sailors who conveyed us to France looked on with amused expressions, occasionally commanding a sufferer to lean farther over the rail so as not to befoul their ship. The vessel stank badly enough as 'twas. When I crossed the sea to France nearly ten years earlier I had suffered no ill effects from the voyage, but the sea was calmer upon that occasion, both leaving Britain and returning. I nearly followed Arthur to the bulwark. By the ninth hour the green hills of France appeared on the horizon before us, and well before darkness settled over the sea our ship joined dozens of others in Calais harbor, awaiting a turn at the wharf to unload.

All was noise and confusion. Men shouted for others to clear a path, and those whose work was with the beasts were loudest of all. Horses neighed and plunged against their grooms. More than one of these men was soundly kicked and I thought my services might be required. The clamor continued until after nightfall, as more ships arrived bearing more nauseous men eager to set foot upon unmoving ground. Do beasts suffer at sea as some men? I wondered if such a malady caused their skittishness.

Arthur and Uctred erected our tent near to the city wall and soon after I fell to sleep to the continuing din of ships being unloaded which carried on the still night air. Were any of the French king's spies about, they would know of our arrival even were they far outside the city wall.

Lord Gilbert and the other great barons who led our campaign were eager to be off as soon as all men, beasts, and supplies reached Calais. But one ship was lost in the crossing, fetching up on the shingle to the south of Calais as her captain tried to beat north across the wind but failed. Four men and three horses were lost, and barrels of oats and salted pork. I'd no thought when I heard of the wreck how great was the loss of a few casks of corn and flesh.

Until we set foot in Calais no man of our company knew where we would go next. We soon learned of our destination. The Duke of Berry had entered Aquitaine, and Prince Edward required of our force that we march with all haste to join him at Bordeaux.

We remained in Calais for two days, repairing carts, setting up traveling forges so as to shoe horses, and organizing the march. None of this was work for me. I wandered about the town, gazed over the sea toward England and my Kate, and kept out of the way of those who had business and needed no advice from me to complete it.

From Calais to Bordeaux is more than three hundred miles. I rode my palfrey alongside Lord Gilbert for most of the first day, and he told me that 'twas his hope to reach Bordeaux by Assumption Day. Such a schedule would require six miles or so each day. I thought such a plan optimistic. Carts break down, and the runcies pulling them tire. Beasts and men go lame, and the French king would surely throw impediments in the way of our march.

At nearly the sixth hour our party crested a hill. From the eminence I could see our force both before and after, snaking its way across the verdant French countryside. Stragglers were lost in the dust of our passage more than a mile to the rear.

Victualers and harbingers went ahead each day to seek food for men and beasts and shelter for the night. For the first week beyond Calais all was well, but as we passed beyond Rouen our difficulties began. We were entering lands ravaged by free companies, where villagers had been robbed of their grain and animals so often that they had developed a system of mutual aid. Whenever an army such as ours approached, folk would warn others in our path, church bells could be heard sounding a warning in distant villages, and when we came to a town or village it would be deserted, inhabitants having fled to fields and forests, barns empty, and goods of value stripped from houses.

Surely there was corn hidden somewhere near these villages, but we were charged with appearing before Bordeaux as soon as possible. We could not take time to scour the countryside seeking meat for men and fodder for beasts.

Our casks of salted pork and stockfish and grain were soon diminished. Our beasts could crop the grass of meadows each night when our march halted – although without oats they would soon weaken and be in no fit condition to draw a cart or bear an armored knight.

Men, however, require provender, and little was to be had. Lord Gilbert required that our company go on short rations. My stomach growled continually for a fortnight until we reached Le Mans and found grain and flesh. The burghers of Le Mans were no doubt true to King Charles, their lord, but did not refuse English silver pennies and shillings.

We departed Le Mans with carts heavy with grain and salted pork and purses lighter. The purses remained lighter, and the carts soon became so. By the time we reached Tours and could replenish our larders we were again on short rations.

And a new affliction began to annoy our travel. We marched through lands of the French king, and to trouble our progress his minions had poisoned wells as we approached. We found dead goats, sheep, boars' heads, even fowl in wells, making the water undrinkable. We could not water our ale, so that also was in short supply. So when our expedition reached Tours we were hungry and thirsty as well.

It was not only houses along our way which were empty.

Village churches were also. No candlesticks, plate, jeweled reliquaries – none of the fixtures common to a church – were to be found. Many of our band sought such plunder, and were out of joint that none was to be had. What is the purpose of war if, in return for the risk, there is no profit?

Three days beyond Tours, shortly after we had halted for the night and set a kettle of pottage to boil, Uctred appeared in the circle of firelight. He had gone to the verge of a nearby wood to relieve himself. I saw him stagger as he came into view, as if stumbling upon some rock unseen in the gathering gloom.

'Twas Arthur who first saw the blood. He sat nearer to the place where Uctred entered our circle of tents. He leaped to his feet and guided his friend close to the fire, the better to see what injury Uctred had received. As the two came near to the blaze I saw also the red flow dripping from Uctred's beard and leaped to offer aid.

I thought at first the groom might have tumbled over a stump or some such thing invisible in the fading light. Not so.

"Three men," he said through thickening lips. "Set upon me when me chauces an' braes was down."

"Who?" Arthur asked.

"Dunno. Too dark."

Most of the gore dripping from Arthur's beard came from his nose. 'Twas likely broken, and for such an injury there is little to be done. I told the fellow to sit upon a bench which had been drawn near the fire, and gently prodded his nose. 'Twas not much out of joint, which he was pleased to learn, and I stopped the bleeding with two small patches of linen from my instruments chest. There was nothing to be done for Uctred's lip, which I could see would, on the morrow, be swollen and discolored to match his nose and eyes.

"You've made an enemy of someone," I said when my ministrations were done. "Who might it be?"

Uctred shrugged. "Try to live peaceable, like, with other folk."

I knew this to be true.

"Don't know who I've angered."

"Three men, you say?" I asked.

"Aye. Think so. 'Twas near to dark, an' I was too busy tryin' to escape their blows an' kicks to count."

"What can you remember of the knaves? Did any seem familiar? Did one wear a garment you recognized, or might recognize if you saw it again?"

Uctred was silent for a moment, then spoke. "One was smallish. No more'n a page, I think, an' he wore a red cap with 'is liripipe coiled queer-like about the side of 'is head, so's it covered an ear."

"Sir Simon's men," Arthur said. He had seen how some in Sir John Trillowe's employ had copied Sir Simon's attempt to conceal his malformed ear.

"Mayhap others have taken to wearing their liripipes in such a fashion," I said. "We must not be hasty in assigning blame."

"Never seen any but them as with Sir Simon wear their caps that way," Arthur growled.

"Nor have I. That does not mean that none do so. Tomorrow morning we will gather a few of Lord Gilbert's men-at-arms and stroll past Sir John's tents. If Uctred sees a page he can recognize we will then plot some way to see justice done."

He did.

Next morn, while some of our party struck our tents Arthur, Uctred, and five other of Lord Gilbert's men joined me in search of Sir John Trillowe's camp. I was unsure of what was to be done if and when we found the villains.

The camp was astir as men stretched, scratched where they itched, rubbed sleep from their eyes, ate and drank what they could find, and made ready for another day's journey.

Sir John's party was but a hundred paces from Lord Gilbert's tents. Sir Simon was seated upon a bench before a rekindled fire and looked up to see who passed. He first scowled, then, as his eyes fell upon Uctred, I saw his face assume a smirk. He turned away and said something over a shoulder.

With the clamor of those breaking camp all about I could

not hear Sir Simon's words, but he must have called to some of his company to attend him, for a few moments later four men appeared from beyond one of the tents which yet stood. These four followed Sir Simon's gaze and watched our approach. One was short and slight, and wore a red cap with liripipe coiled so as to cover an ear.

Much like Sir Simon's.

I turned to Uctred. "Yon lad with the red cap... was he one who attacked you, you think?"

"Could be. Not many who have red caps, an' fewer who wind their liripipes in such fashion," he mumbled through thick lips.

"Wait here," I said to Uctred. "You've taken enough blows recently." To the others with me I said, "Do not draw your daggers unless they draw first, but be ready."

"What have you in mind?" Arthur said. "Shall we deal with them as they did Uctred?" His tone indicated that he hoped I would answer affirmatively.

We seven approached Sir Simon's five and when he saw that we drew near with thin lips and scowling brows he stood and called his men to come near.

"I give you good day, Master Hugh," Sir Simon said with mock courtesy. "How may I serve Lord Gilbert's... bailiff?" The use of my title in such a fashion was to put me in my place. It was not successful.

I placed hands on hips and assumed a resolute posture. I am too slight to assume this well, but Arthur, at my side, did likewise and is more successful at threatening with only stance and gaze.

"One of Lord Gilbert's men," I said calmly, "was attacked last eve. Your men were responsible."

"My men? Surely not. We are peaceable fellows, are we not?"

Sir Simon grinned and turned to the four who now stood close behind him as he spoke. I saw his hand fall to his sheathed dagger. "You are mistaken."

"No mistake. Your quarrel is with me, not that man," I

said, nodding toward Uctred. "You lost a fair maid to me, were required to pay for my house, which you destroyed, and have now a misshapen ear – better than no ear at all, which would be true had I not sewn the appendage back to your ungrateful skull."

Color rose in Sir Simon's cheeks as I reminded him and his men of his past losses, most of which were due to his own blunders. Decisions have consequences.

Sir Simon then made another foolish decision, which, as I look back upon the event, I see I had goaded him to do. May the Lord Christ forgive me. Sir Simon drew his dagger. Instantly ten other men did the same; Sir Simon's four men and the six of Lord Gilbert's company who stood behind me. I alone left my dagger sheathed, although I was ready to draw, for my blood was up.

"Aye," Sir Simon said, "and 'tis you I shall deal with."

"You have already tried." I rubbed my chin. "My injury has healed. But if you come near me with that dagger we are seven to your five. The odds are not in your favor, and when the fight is past and you lie in the mud with slashes about your body, you can seek another surgeon, for I will not stitch you back together another time."

"Bah. What do I care for that?"

Sir Simon's reply was more confident than the expressions upon the faces of his minions. I saw them glance toward us as we stood opposed to them, and then to each other. Their valiant demeanor began to fade from resolute to anxious. Arthur, standing at my side with a dagger in his hand and a frown upon his face, will do that to a man.

"Uctred's nose is broken," I said calmly. "Someone must pay for the injury."

"When you find the guilty man, require satisfaction of him," Sir Simon said. "Till then, leave us or suffer the consequences of your impudence."

"I have found the men. Uctred's nose is worth two shillings, I think. He will have the coins of you, as you and your father are responsible for the deeds of your men."

"You will have two shillings of me when the Holy Father offers his chair to that heretic Wycliffe."

"Two shillings will be less costly than losing another ear," Arthur said from behind my shoulder.

This was more than a knight could bear from a mere groom. Sir Simon spoke something I could not understand, so enraged was he, and leaped toward Arthur. Another mistake.

Arthur ducked the blow, and as Sir Simon passed him, he swept his left hand across the back of the knight's head. Sir Simon went to his knees, stunned, and his dagger flew from his hand.

His men crouched, ready to come to his aid. One or two stepped forward, but then considered the armed men who opposed them and hesitated.

I plucked Sir Simon's dagger from the mud and studied it as he regained his feet.

"A fine dagger," I said, turning the weapon in my hand. "Worth two shillings, perhaps more."

Sir Simon blinked in the morning sunlight and considered his condition. His bluster had vanished. He stepped back, then looked over his shoulder to discover what aid he could expect. He found little.

"This will be returned to you when Uctred receives his two shillings," I said, then turned my back to Sir Simon so that he would understand that I did not fear him. Not when I had Arthur and six other brawny men at hand.

Sir Simon stood speechless as I returned to the path where Uctred waited. I assume he stood. He said nothing and I doubt that he resumed his seat upon the bench, but I did not turn to see that this was so.

One by one Arthur and the other of Lord Gilbert's men followed me, but unlike me they did not turn their backs to Sir Simon and his men, nor did they sheathe their daggers. Just in case.

Chapter 4

By the time we returned to Lord Gilbert's encampment the tents were struck, beasts harnessed to carts, and our cohort ready to take to the road. Lord Gilbert, unaware of recent events, mounted his ambler, waved to the knights, men-at-arms, and carters to follow, and we set off behind the train of Sir Henry Thorpe. Sir John Trillowe's party was somewhere behind us upon the road that morn, and I confess to peering over my shoulder more than once when I thought I heard hoofbeats approaching more rapidly than should be. Sir Simon's dagger I had placed secure in my instruments chest, which was now in a cart otherwise laden with arrows, pikes, and poleaxes.

'Twas near to midday when I saw Sir John Trillowe ride past me and continue till he was abreast Lord Gilbert. An animated conversation followed – animated on Sir John's part. He gestured vigorously with his right hand to emphasize his words, and twice looked over a shoulder in my direction. I smiled a polite greeting.

Lord Gilbert and Sir John are not friends. I know of no past quarrel between them; they simply do not care for each other's company. From my experience there are many others who share Lord Gilbert's antipathy.

Sir John rode beside Lord Gilbert for perhaps a mile, then yanked most cruelly upon his horse's reins, spinning the beast about in the road. Sir John spurred the beast to a gallop and thundered past without another glance toward me.

A moment later Lord Gilbert turned in his saddle and beckoned me to join him.

"Sir John is displeased with you," Lord Gilbert said when I drew alongside him. "Of course," he chuckled, "you have much fellowship. Sir John is seldom pleased with anyone."

I said nothing, awaiting Lord Gilbert's instruction in the matter of Sir Simon's dagger, which I was sure was the cause of Sir John's lively conversation with my employer.

"Where is Sir Simon's dagger?" Lord Gilbert asked.

"Safe in my instruments chest."

"Hah... a good place for a blade. Worth two shillings, you think?"

"Thereabouts," I replied.

"And you are sure 'twas Sir Simon's men who attacked Uctred?" Lord Gilbert had heard rumours of the blows Uctred had taken. A purpled face will be spoken of in camp.

"Aye. He identified one of them."

"What if Sir Simon will not pay two shillings to recover his dagger?"

"I will give the weapon to Uctred. He may do with it as he wishes. If Sir Simon does pay I will give the two shillings to Uctred to ease the pain of his wounds."

"Why would Sir Simon's men set upon Uctred?" Lord Gilbert asked.

"He is seen with me, and wears your livery, so is easily identified. Sir Simon is much like his father. He can sustain a grudge longer than most men."

"Ah, just so. He courted Kate, did he not, and then burned Galen House when you took her from him? Well, your actions this day will not have soothed his wrath. Best you keep a close watch for Sir Simon or his men."

"So I intend. I have already met him unaware and suffered for the encounter."

Lord Gilbert stared at me and raised one eyebrow, a thing he does when curious about some matter. I tried in years past to emulate the expression but gave it up.

"Wonder why your Kate encouraged Sir Simon's suit," Lord Gilbert mused.

"As did I," I replied. "Shortly after we wed she spoke of it. I did not press her about the matter. She felt the need to explain, I think.

"Sir John was sheriff of Oxford at the time, and to gain a return on the fee he paid to the king to acquire the office, he was fining the burghers of Oxford for every violation, real or imagined. Kate feared that if she rejected Sir Simon's suit her father would suffer financial loss at Sir John's hand. She was much distressed, finding Sir Simon repugnant, but worried for her father's business if she refused Sir Simon's suit.

"When King Edward dismissed Sir John because of the burghers' complaints against him Kate was no longer compelled to consent to Sir Simon's court."

"Ah," Lord Gilbert said. "So that's why he took revenge by burning Galen House?"

"Aye. Now I must watch that he doesn't seek revenge for his dagger."

"And his humiliation before his men," Lord Gilbert added.

"Sir John rode away just now seeming much annoyed," I said.

"Aye. He demanded return of the dagger. I told him that I knew nothing of the matter, but would speak to you of it. I have done so."

"You did not promise the dagger's return?"

"Nay. Sir John was not pleased."

"I admit that I took the dagger without measuring the consequences," I said. "Sir Simon was an enemy before this day. He is even more so now."

"Will you return it, then, to soothe his ire?"

"I will think on it. Whether or not returning the dagger will moderate his anger, I do not know. But Uctred deserves some recompense for the pain he suffers."

"Aye, he does. And if Sir John and Sir Simon are not made responsible for what their men do to one of mine, I am made to appear weak, unable to defend those who serve me. Keep the dagger until he pays two shillings. But go nowhere alone."

I did not need Lord Gilbert's advice upon this matter, for I had already resolved to keep companions about me. I touched my cap, bowed in the saddle, and reined my palfrey to a halt beside the road until Lord Gilbert's knights had passed and I could rejoin the procession with grooms, archers, and men-at-arms. Lord Gilbert had, in the past month, occasionally summoned me to ride in company with him, but I thought it presumptuous to do so without invitation.

Uctred's nose and eyes were fading from purple to greenish yellow when, four days past Assumption Day, we crested a hill and saw before us the walls of Bordeaux. We pitched tents beside the main gate to the city and awaited news of the Duke of Berry. 'Twas not long coming.

But a few days before we made Bordeaux the duke had received the surrender of Limoges. Prince Edward was furious at the perfidy of the Bishop of Limoges, who, men said, was responsible for giving the city to the French. We would not remain long at Bordeaux. The prince intended to march on Limoges forthwith and recover his lost possession.

Great men had gathered at Bordeaux to aid Prince Edward. His brothers, John of Gaunt and Edmund of Langley, were present, as was that great warrior the Captal de Buch, and also the Earl of Pembroke, John Hastings.

Lord Gilbert said our force now numbered more than three thousand men: knights, archers, and men-at-arms. Prince Edward demanded that this force be ready to descend upon Limoges by St. Bartholomew's Day, but in part due to the prince's illness the army did not begin its march till nearly a week after its intended departure. In the intervening days, much to my surprise and with trepidation, I was called to wait upon the ailing prince.

Prince Edward had not been well since returning from his successful, if expensive, campaign to Spain to restore Peter of Castile to his throne. Many physicians had been called to the prince, but none could cure him, not even his personal leech, William Blackwater, who, I was told, is paid forty pounds each year to care for Edward.

My name was mentioned to Prince Edward whilst Lord Gilbert was in conversation with him. He required that I be brought to him, saying to Lord Gilbert that, as long as no physician could make him well, he might try what a surgeon could do for him.

I heard Lord Gilbert tell me of the prince's command with mixed feelings. I was eager to meet such a great knight, but feared bringing him bad news. And this I was sure I must do. If the best physicians could not cure Edward, a surgeon would not. Nevertheless, 'twas an honor to be called into the presence of the Prince of Wales. What would my father say, could he have guessed that his youngest son would be presented to royalty? And when I tell my Kate she will surely be impressed by her husband's rise.

Some days, I learned, the prince was so weak he could not mount a horse, and must be carried from place to place upon a litter. When I entered his palace, accompanied by Lord Gilbert, I did not know if I would find him seated or abed.

Edward was seated, attended by valets and aides, and took our bows with a wave of his hand. I had never seen my employer bow to another man. But I had never before seen him enter the presence of royalty.

"My Lord Gilbert," the prince began, "has told me that you are a cunning surgeon. For four years I have been unwell. I have consumed herbs and physics and observed odd diets. Some learned doctors say the humors are out of balance and I must eat more meat. Others suggest I eat apples and berries and such stuff to restore my body to stability. One physician said I must take more wine, another said I must drink none. What say you, Master Hugh?"

"I am no physician," I replied. "Should you fall from your horse and break an arm I am your man, but I have no training for the diseases which plague mankind."

"Hah... if no man can cure me of this malady I may become so feeble that I will topple from my beast. I will then call for you. As for your training, the physicians who have attended me are all scholars, so they claim, but for all their knowledge are unable to make me well. You can do no worse."

The prince's logic was unassailable. Of course, when a man is to become the next King of England his logic is always unassailable, and those who would disagree will find themselves in uneasy embarrassment.

"You have been ill for four years?" I asked. "What do you suffer? How does the ailment show itself?"

"In every way," the prince replied. "Often a bloody flux, and

44

my arse so sore I cannot sit a horse. One day a fever, next a chill so that I wrap myself in blankets, in Aquitaine, in the summer! I pass wind so foul that folk do not wish to be in the same chamber with me."

"What do the physicians say?"

"I told you," Edward replied with exasperation in his voice. 'Tis best not to exasperate a prince. I told myself I must measure my words more carefully.

"Oh, aye... that your humors are unbalanced."

"Just so. What say you?"

"Nothing," I shrugged. "Mayhap they speak true. But I will be frank. I've never seen a man ill as you are who regained his health because a physician altered his diet from hot to cold or wet to dry, or the other way 'round."

"You say that the leeches who offer advice and take my coin for it are knaves?"

"Perhaps they have seen their counsel succeed with other patients," I said.

"But you've not seen it so?"

"Nay," I replied.

"What, then, is to become of me? Am I to meet the Lord Christ soon?"

"I cannot say, m'lord. There are herbs which may reduce your suffering, if not work a cure."

"Oh? What?"

"Tansy, thyme, cress, and bramble leaves crushed and made into an oily paste, mixed then with wine. And an oil from the roots of fennel."

"You have offered such to others and seen them relieved?"

"Nay, m'lord. I've heard of good success with these, but surgeons are not called upon to deal with complaints these herbs may soothe."

"Until now, eh?"

"Aye. Until now."

"Hmmm. An honest man. Most physicians brought to me promise a cure. They assign me remedies and take their pay, and after all I am no better. Worse, indeed, sometimes. What about you? What is your fee for advising me to take... what herbs again?"

"Tansy, thyme, cress, bramble leaves, and the root of fennel. These are claimed to reduce wind. And I ask no fee from those I cannot serve."

"Hah. A man who will not enrich himself at my expense. Very well, I will send for my leech and have the fellow prepare the herbs you suggest."

Prince Edward turned to a valet and said, "Fetch Dr. Blackwater. I pay him enough," Edward said to me. "He can collect herbs and pound them to earn his wages."

Lord Gilbert and I bowed our way out of Prince Edward's pavilion, and as we departed I saw the prince helped from his chair and taken toward a couch. Evidently he had mastered his weakness long enough for my interview, but was now required to lie down. I hoped that the herbs I had suggested would serve to better his weakness. If they did, what then? Would my reputation be aided? Would the prince ask me to serve in his entourage? Would I want to do so, were he to ask? And if such an invitation came, what would Kate think? Would she want to leave Galen House and travel at the whim of Prince Edward? Would I?

*

Whilst we waited outside the walls of Bordeaux, men readied themselves and their weapons for battle. Archers sharpened already keen arrows on portable wheels and men-at-arms did likewise with pikes and axes. When there was nothing remaining to be done men drank too much ale and wine and gambled at nine man morris or dice. I care little for gambling, drunkenness does not appeal to me, and I had no weapons to sharpen. I was bored. I took to wandering about the city, comparing it to London and other great cities I have seen. A man could do worse than make a home in Bordeaux. Perhaps this is why so many of English royalty have spent time there.

Four days after our arrival at Bordeaux a man of Sir John

Trillowe's company approached our tents. He asked for me, and when I stood before my tent he opened his pouch, produced two shillings, and demanded the return of Sir Simon's dagger. I remembered the fellow. John de Boys. He had accompanied Sir Simon at Leeds Castle on the evening when Sir Simon struck me.

I went to my chest, drew forth the dagger, and made the exchange. It was a fine blade. Perhaps I should have required three shillings for its return. The youth took Sir Simon's dagger, glared at me, and stalked off. Perhaps the fellow was chosen for the task because of his excellent scowl. I have seldom received a more venomous glance.

Word of the groom's appearance passed quickly through Lord Gilbert's tents and men gathered to see what the fellow's arrival might mean. Uctred was among these. I gave him the two shillings and he grinned.

"Worth a busted nose," he said.

A few minutes after the groom had left with Sir Simon's dagger we heard an uproar from a distant part of the camp. Bored men always seek entertainment, and the tumult, distant though it was, promised amusement. We left our tents and sought the source of the racket.

Twenty or so men were battering each other in an open space between two clusters of tents. One group wore Sir John Trillowe's livery, the other wore Sir Henry Morley's colors. No daggers flashed, but men beat upon each other with fists, lengths of firewood, and kicks to the ribs of fallen foes. One man entered the fray with a rock larger than my fist and threw it with all the force he could muster toward an opponent. He missed, and the missile bounced harmlessly from the wall of a tent.

Dozens of men soon gathered about the bloodied combatants, but most chose to encourage the contest rather than end it. Eventually a few of the less pugnacious of the brawlers began to fall away from the field of battle, and others of Sir John's and Sir Henry's men who were not involved stepped between the exhausted few whose dander was yet up, and brought the spectacle to an end.

Quiet returned to the encampment, and we who had been briefly diverted from the boredom of waiting drifted back to our tents.

"Wonder what caused that?" Arthur said as we came to our place.

"Heard one fella say that Sir Simon was cheatin' at dice," one of Lord Gilbert's archers said. How he would do that I knew not, but knowing Sir Simon, if there were a way to defraud another at dice, he would find it. There is, and he did. Perhaps I was prejudiced against the man.

Chapter 5

Two days later, with no more fights to entertain us, we learned that the army would move next morn for Limoges. The journey was not far. Most were pleased to be on the way to our destination, for the sooner Limoges was dealt with the sooner we could return to England. But it was annoying to give up the comforts of the camp we had made, and pack all for the move to Limoges.

On the second day of travel, when I had left the road to seek a private place to relieve myself, I saw Sir Simon Trillowe and the man who had ransomed his dagger riding past, side by side. Comrades, evidently, joking and laughing as they rode. But then the laughter changed abruptly to shouts and curses. From what I knew of Sir Simon's temper, I thought it likely that his friend had said something to which Sir Simon took offense. From forty or so paces away I heard the friend shout in response, "You'll not find another." Another what? I wondered. Sir Simon then turned his back upon the fellow and spurred his beast ahead. I managed to circle ahead of the quarreling pair and rejoin Lord Gilbert's cohort without them noticing me. I think.

Ten days later we arrived before the walls of Limoges and erected our tents in a circle about the city. Prince Edward was so unwell that he traveled in a litter, which must have been mortifying to so great a knight.

The French knew we were coming and, as before, had poisoned wells and emptied barns. Few villagers remained in the towns we passed, most folk preferring to abandon their homes rather than suffer the injuries a passing army might inflict upon them. These were inhabitants of Aquitaine, an English possession, but no man among us was ready to guarantee their loyalty. Such folk tend to give fealty to the sovereign with the most powerful army, and men of the countryside through which we passed had not yet decided which prince that might be, Edward or Charles.

When we arrived at Limoges we learned that the Duke of Berry was away. When he had discovered the size of the army which approached he took his force from Limoges rather than be besieged in the town. Spies told Prince Edward that fewer than one hundred and fifty knights and men-at-arms remained in the city, along with folk of the town, numbering about two thousand.

The city is found where two rivers converge, and is located between the two just before they join. To take the city an army must either cross one of the rivers or fight its way down the peninsula between the streams to approach the walls. Prince John decided to build a plank bridge across the smaller of the streams, so as to approach the city wall directly. I am no soldier, but I admit that I thought at the time that we had undertaken a difficult task. Limoges's walls were high and strong. In my ignorance of military things I thought that, given a choice, I would prefer to be inside the walls defending the place, rather than outside, preparing to attack. This is why I am a surgeon, not a knight.

So long as the walls of Limoges stood, one hundred and fifty warriors might successfully defend the place against three thousand. The walls must come down. We had no trebuchet or mangonel with which to batter the ramparts to rubble, but Prince Edward had a weapon nearly as potent: tin miners from Cornwall.

Lord Gilbert explained the process to me. The miners would dig a great tunnel under a likely section of the wall. As they progressed, timbers would be placed so as to support the excavation and the wall, and a shelter of heavy planks would be built and shoved to the base of the wall to protect those who labored to undermine the foundation. Without such a structure soldiers high upon the wall could pour down upon the miners rocks, arrows, even boiling water.

When the shaft was deep enough, the cavity would be filled with dry brush and perhaps a cask or two of lard, and set ablaze. When fire consumed the supporting timbers the city wall might collapse, if all went according to plan – which in war, Lord Gilbert said, almost never happens.

So whilst the tin miners plied their picks and spades, there was little for others to do but wait to learn if the labor would be fruitful. Lord Gilbert's tents were pitched a safe distance from any French crossbow bolts, just over a slight hill beyond the river and the temporary bridge. I felt safe enough there, and ventured each day to the top of the rise to watch the miners from a distance. On the third day of digging I was called to treat a miner who had received a crossbow bolt in his shoulder. The fellow had unwisely peered around the side of the timber shelter while resting from his labor, and a crossbowman glancing through a merlon saw him and loosed a bolt.

The bolt had penetrated the fellow's collarbone, and was most troublesome to extract. Doing so caused the man much pain, but he understood that he could not spend the remainder of his life going about with a shaft embedded in his shoulder. Well, he could, I suppose, but that would mean the remainder of his life would be brief. I might have given the miner a draught of ale with pounded hemp seeds, but such a palliative requires an hour or so to do its work, and I thought the man would prefer to have the bolt extracted sooner rather than later. And pounded hemp seeds have but small effect in such cases. Removing the bolt from such a wound will cause agony, no matter what herbs the sufferer may consume.

With a scalpel I cut away the man's kirtle – he had worn no tunic or cotehardie whilst at work in the tunnel. Three of the miner's fellows held him to a table whilst I grasped the shaft and yanked it free. The miner gasped and would have thrashed about, but miners tend to be sturdy men and his friends held him fast till the wave of pain passed.

I held the bolt before the sufferer's eyes and when he focused upon it and realized what it was I saw relief flood his expression, and then a smile as he understood that the worst was past. Unless the wound should fester.

A wound bathed in wine heals most readily, although no

man knows why this is so. I splashed some of Lord Gilbert's malmsey on a swatch of linen cloth and thoroughly cleansed the puncture. Due to the nature of such a wound it bled little. Using a length of old linen I made a sling and told the miner that he should leave his arm immobile for a week or perhaps longer. When he could flex his shoulder with little pain he might then dispense with the sling. Pain can be a friend, a companion which tells a man that he should cease whatever it is he is doing which is causing his ache. The fellow did not seem unhappy that his labor in the shaft must end for a time.

For the next several days I did not see Sir Simon or the friend he had sent to retrieve his dagger. His absence caused me no distress.

Chapter 6

On the fifth day outside Limoges, soon after dawn, one of Sir John Trillowe's grooms found Sir Simon. He was discovered head down, drowned in a poisoned well in Couzeix, a village but half a mile from the camp.

I admit that this report did not cause me sorrow. The man had harbored much ill will toward me, and unless his father or his grooms chose to continue his malice, I saw a future in which I would no longer need to concern myself with schemes Sir Simon might have plotted against me.

'Twas Arthur who heard of Sir Simon's death whilst he traveled the camp, and brought word to me. He smiled as he told me, and I admit that my features likely also reflected joy. May the Lord Christ forgive me. We are told we must not take pleasure in the misfortune of those who would do us harm. Few men are able to obey such an injunction. I am one of these. Three months past I read in my Bible that we are to do good to those who do us injury, and not return evil for evil.

How can a man do so? I began to wonder if possessing my own Bible was a wise thing. Before I owned a copy of the Scriptures my knowledge and understanding of Holy Writ was incomplete. Now I know better what I must do and not do, think and not think, in order to please the Lord Christ. My life was simpler when I knew less. Even the scholars at Oxford under whom I studied usually chose to ignore the Lord Christ's hard words.

"Drunk on too much wine, I'd guess," Arthur concluded. "Why else go head first into a well all know is poisoned? An' no man needs wells anyway."

This was so. Two rivers flowed past the walls of Limoges: La Vienne and L'Aurence. No man need seek a well for water. Why the French troubled themselves to cast some dead creature into such a well, when a man had but to carry a bucket a few hundred paces from the camp for all the water he might want, no man could guess. It is difficult to understand the behavior of the French. I gave the matter no more thought.

Until the ninth hour. A page came to me and announced that Lord Gilbert would speak to me. I found him at his tent. He was not alone. Sir John Trillowe was there, his face purple with wrath.

I bowed to the two men, doffed my cap, and bid them "Good day."

"'Tis no good day," Sir John bellowed. "And you know well why 'tis not."

"Aye," I agreed. "I have heard of Sir Simon's death."

"Heard! Why would you need to hear of it? You slew him."

The accusation stunned me. My response to the charge, taken aback as I was, did nothing to convince Sir John that it was unjust. My mouth opened and closed, but I seemed unable to find appropriate words.

"What say you to this charge?" Lord Gilbert said.

"Not so, m'lord. I have slain no man."

"You were seen with him last night," Sir John said. "You and that ox-like groom who goes about with you."

"Seen? What? Attacking Sir Simon? The man who says so lies."

"You hated my son. All who know you know this to be true."

"Nay. I hate no man. 'Twas the other way 'round. Sir Simon hated me, and tried to do me harm whenever he could."

"Hah. You say so yourself. Reason enough to slay him. You feared his wrath against you for your malfeasance."

"Malfeasance? What harm did I to Sir Simon?"

"His ear. You made him a mark of ridicule."

"He would have been more maligned had I not saved his ear. I regret that I could not make it as good as God made it, but without my skill he would have had no ear at all."

"Bah... what you say is of no consequence. You and the other were seen walking with Sir Simon last night, just after sunset. No man saw him again till he was discovered in the well."

54

"How long past sunset?" I asked.

"What difference?" Sir John said.

"How long past?" Lord Gilbert repeated. I believe he followed my thought. "Before midnight?"

"Aye, before midnight."

"The moon is in its last quarter," I said. "There was no moonlight till past midnight. How could your witness have seen who was with Sir Simon on such a dark night?"

Sir John swallowed deeply. I saw his adam's apple work. Here was information he had not considered.

"Perhaps," Lord Gilbert said gently, "you should seek this witness and make yourself more certain of matters before you accuse my surgeon of felony. 'Twas cloudy last night as well. Even light from the stars was dimmed. Did your witness carry a torch?"

Lord Gilbert's words were temperate, yet spoken in such a tone that Sir John was sure to understand that Lord Gilbert was not pleased that I had been so accused.

"I see I will find no justice here," Sir John complained. "Prince Edward will hear of this."

"Did Sir Simon die of drowning... in the well?" I asked.

"You should know. You put him there."

"Was there sign of attack? Was he wounded? Perhaps if I could examine the corpse I might tell you more of this death."

"What?" Sir John shouted. "Never! You have slain my son. You will not touch him now!"

And with those words Sir John spun on his heel and stalked from the tent. I watched him go, then turned, speechless, to Lord Gilbert.

"Sir Simon," Lord Gilbert said, "was a danger. His father is more so. He was once a sheriff, even though the king turned him out for his greed. Prince Edward will consider this charge. Sir John will gain a hearing, I fear."

"What do you suggest?"

"Find who did murder, if that is what happened, so blame cannot be fixed to you. You truly did no harm to Sir Simon?"

"None, m'lord. I was asleep upon my pallet when Sir Simon went into the well. If he had too much wine last eve, he likely plunged in while drunk."

"Oh, aye... likely. 'Twill be another matter to persuade Sir John of that."

"I would need to ask of Sir John's knights and grooms and men-at-arms if Sir Simon drank excessively last eve. And I must speak to the witness who claims to have seen me with Sir Simon. Which of these would answer truthfully if doing so would absolve me of felony against Sir John's wishes?"

"Likely none. You will need to seek truth somewhere other than Sir John's camp."

Where that might be I could not guess, but I thought a good beginning might be made by visiting the well where Sir Simon had been found. What I might find there I did not know, but a charge of murder might lead to a hempen rope and a grave in France. I must discover some evidence that I had slain no man. Proving a man guilty of some felony is difficult enough. Proving innocence can be even more onerous. But if the incentive is one's own life, even arduous labor is no obstacle to a search for truth.

I departed Lord Gilbert's tent, went to my own, and buckled my dagger to my belt. Did the Lord Christ really demand that His followers turn the other cheek if it was likely that both cheeks would be carved away by some evil fellow armed with a blade? There is much difference between a slap and a slash. I must seek counsel of Master Wycliffe when next I see him. But until then I intended to be armed at all times.

Arthur approached as I fixed the sheath to my belt. He raised his eyebrows.

"I have just returned from Lord Gilbert," I said. "Sir John Trillowe has accused me, and you as well, of slaying Sir Simon."

Arthur had already his dagger upon his belt, and reached a hand to the hilt as I spoke.

"Lord Gilbert don't believe 'im, does 'e?"

"Nay. Sir John claims we were seen walking with Sir Simon after dark, but before midnight. Such a claim is absurd for two reasons: there was no moon to light the night till past midnight, and why would Sir Simon be about late at night with me, a man he hated?"

Arthur glanced at my dagger. "You think Sir John will send some of 'is men to attack you... us?"

"It has crossed my mind. Probably not while we are within the camp. 'Twould cause too great a tumult and bring all of Lord Gilbert's men down upon them. And if he can convince Prince Edward that I did murder, he will not need to send men to assail me. I will do the sheriff's dance."

"But keep a dagger close by, eh, just in case?"

"Just so. And I intend to leave the camp for an hour or two."

"Leave? Where will you go?"

"To the well where Sir Simon was found. Lord Gilbert's advice is to find the cause of Sir Simon's death, be it felony or mischance, so as to deflect Sir John's wrath."

"I've nothing better to do this day. I'll go also."

"And seek Uctred. The stronger a band of men is, the less likely they will need to prove it."

Arthur returned shortly with Uctred and two of Lord Gilbert's men-at-arms, William and Alfred. I briefly explained to the newcomers what we were about to do and why, and we set out for Couzeix.

The village was just beyond a hill which bordered the camp, so we reached the place in but a few minutes. It was, like other villages nearby, apparently empty of inhabitants and their beasts and fowl. The village was an English possession, and our army was English, but no villager would risk the assumption that his property would not be plundered.

There were twelve houses, a stone church, and several barns in Couzeix. The village was not prosperous. All of the houses and barns needed new thatching, and the church windows were few and small, to save the cost of glass. Couzeix is near the boundary between the lands of the French king and English claims. Such a place will often see marauding armies as contending forces battle for advantage. Treaties of peace between the kings of

England and France are regularly signed and as often violated. Which is why I was standing near a well in France many miles from my Kate and our daughters.

The well was covered, and stood in a small grassy common in nearly the center of the village. I looked about but could see no other well, and thought it unlikely a village of a dozen houses would need two wells. And this well was fairly large for such a mean village. 'Twas as great across as I am tall, and a little more. Here, then, was where Sir Simon was found. Did he die here, also? Or did some fellow pitch his corpse into the well, assuming that as it was known to be poisoned, no man would drop a bucket into the well and Sir Simon would be undiscovered for many days?

I led my cohorts to the well and peered in. The roof covering it darkened the shaft, so that if there was any clue to be found it would be invisible to any but a close examination. I had no desire to descend into the black hole, so contented myself with a glance into its depths. I saw a dim reflection from the surface of the water, perhaps six or seven paces below ground. If a man fell that far head first he might die of a broken head, depending upon the depth of the water, rather than drowning. What difference? Such a mishap would kill in one way or another. The reflection was broken by a shadow of some sort. The creature which was tossed into the well was yet there, rotting in its depths.

I stood back from the well and circled it, examining the stones which lined the lip of the well, and the soil around it. Many men had visited the well and made shoe prints in the dirt. These were likely Sir John's men who found Sir Simon and came to draw him from the well.

A bucket and a coil of worn hempen rope lay nearby. No man would have used the bucket for many days, surely, for it seemed to me likely that the well was defiled a day or two before our army came to the place. Why drop a bucket into a poisoned well?

I was about to pass by the bucket, giving it no further thought, when an anomaly caught my eye.

The morning sun illuminated a reddened spot on the otherwise brown wood. I knelt to study this stain more closely.

A surgeon sees much blood, both fresh and dried. Arthur saw me bend to inspect the bucket, saw also the red-brown smear, and spoke.

"Blood, you think?"

"Aye. Some man swung that bucket against some other man's head, I think." I've been wrong before.

Arthur grasped the bail and gave the bucket a swing about his head.

"A man could deliver a solid blow with this," he said. I agreed. I would not like to receive such a stroke, especially if Arthur or one like him delivered it.

The village appeared deserted. Appearances may be deceiving. I thought that perhaps some resident, perhaps elderly or infirm, or both, might at that moment be peering at me through a slit in the skin covering a window. And if so he might have done the same the night before and seen or heard some disturbance at the well.

A wise commander does not divide his force, so Lord Gilbert has said. So I did not split our small band to save time investigating the apparently empty houses clustered about the common, but kept my company together.

None of the houses had locks, such being too expensive, surely, for the residents of such a place, most of whom owned little worth stealing. We entered three houses, found them bare of possessions, and then came to the church.

I thought that perhaps the village priest or a clerk, trusting his office to protect him, might have remained behind when his flock fled. There was little light in the church. Candles had long since sputtered out, there evidently being no one to tend them, and the few small windows gave scant illumination. So I nearly missed seeing the crone who crouched behind the font.

The woman wore a ragged cotehardie and threw her bony hands up before her face as if to defend from a blow when she saw that I had discovered her hiding place. There followed a raspy flow of words in some Gascon dialect which was nearly indecipherable to my English ears. I had spent a year in Paris studying surgery, and knew the French language well – or as well as any Englishman can comprehend the tongue – but the rapid utterances I now heard bore little resemblance to the speech of Paris.

After a minute or two of this the old woman fell silent, exhausted, and huddled close to the base of the font, as if the holy water within might protect her if I had felonious designs against her.

"What did she say?" Arthur asked.

"I know not," I shrugged.

I knelt beside the woman and spoke slowly and softly. Slowly so she might understand my French, and softly so that she might be reassured that I had no wish to harm her. "Where are the folk of Couzeix?"

The crone's eyes darted from me to the porch door and back again, as if she considered fleeing. I thought mayhap she did not understand French spoken by an Englishman, so was about to repeat the question when she replied, slowly. I understood most of her words.

Villagers, she said, had fled before the approach of Prince Edward's army. Some who had kin in villages far enough from Limoges to think themselves safe, but near enough to flee to, had gone to seek refuge with these relatives. There were few who did so. Others, not so fortunate, were hiding in the forest. All, wherever they had gone, had evidently taken with them whatever of value they owned, for the houses we had entered before reaching the church were stripped clean.

"If all have deserted the village, why are you here?" I asked.

I believe the woman understood me better than I did her. She answered without requiring that I repeat the question.

Her son was dead of plague twenty years, she said. Her daughter-in-law had allowed her to remain with the family, but the two women did not enjoy a harmonious life together. So when the younger woman fled the town with her children, she refused to take her mother-in-law with her. The family had no cart in which the older woman could ride, nor a beast to pull such. One so aged and infirm would slow the escape.

The church, she was told, would be a sanctuary. Even the barbaric English would not slay an old woman in a church and defile it so. The woman was left with water, a wooden porringer of barley pottage, and a promise that her family would return for her as soon as they could safely do so. I looked beside the woman and saw that the porringer was nearly empty, and what remained was coagulated to the consistency of lard. The woman would starve before Prince Edward's tin miners could collapse the wall of Limoges, unless more pottage was soon brought to her. It would be. The woman had evidently not been abandoned. Someone would bring her food soon, though the crone did not divulge this.

Beside the porringer I saw a wooden cup of water. Where could this have come from? The well was poisoned and I was unsure if the old woman could have tottered to it even had the water been pure. I asked her of the source.

A cistern, the crone said, behind the reeve's house, held rainwater. Each night, well after darkness had fallen, she hoisted herself to her feet using a crude crutch which lay upon the flags beside her, went to the reeve's privy, then filled the cup from the cistern and returned to hide behind the font. Given her feeble condition, I thought that such an excursion would take her an hour or so, depending upon the distance she must hobble.

"Which house?" I asked, and when she described it I sent Uctred to learn if the tale was true – if there was indeed a cistern where rainwater could be had.

Whilst Uctred was away I asked another question: "How could you see to find a cistern in the dark of night?"

"Waited till moon was up," the crone said. Which meant that she had not departed the church the previous night until past midnight.

"Did you see men about the well this morning? Or hear them speak?"

She had, but claimed the disease of the ears, and feared

discovery, so did not peer from a window to learn what had brought men to an abandoned village. The church was a fair distance from the well, so their voices were faint, and in any case, even had she heard them well, she spoke no English. I wondered if the men whose voices she heard might have been French, natives from nearby villages, come to loot what little remained in Couzeix. The crone said, "Nay. They was close enough to hear was it my tongue they spoke."

"You have but little pottage remaining," I said. "I will send more."

I did not know what else to do for the woman. I could not return to the camp with her, and she would not return to her house to be discovered, perhaps, by bored soldiers seeking sport.

The woman spoke again. The men who had entered the village shortly after dawn, she said, might be the same who had come in the night.

At that moment Uctred returned and verified that there was indeed a cistern behind the house the crone had described. 'Twas the most substantial dwelling in the village, and behind it was a shed with a board roof which funneled water to a cask. So Uctred said.

"Men came in the night?" I said. "How many?"

The woman could not say. They spoke softly, she said, as if the village was inhabited and they did not wish to awaken it.

"Was there an argument? A fight?" I asked.

The crone pled ignorance, due to faulty ears. I thought it reasonable that, if she heard men speaking softly, she would have heard a dispute which resulted in one man smiting another with a bucket. If the woman did not hear such a brawl, perhaps Sir Simon's death happened elsewhere, or the bucket had nothing to do with it. Or perhaps the crone's hearing was so weak that what she took for a whispered conversation was a heated argument.

If a blow was not delivered in the night near to the well, whence came the smear of blood on the bucket? Perhaps 'twas not blood. What, then? And if blood, mayhap not from a man but of a beast. Why would the blood of a beast stain a bucket used for a village well? The visit to Couzeix was producing more questions than answers.

I could think of no more questions for the woman. However, I knew where she could be found if I thought of more later. In her frail condition she would not travel far.

We returned to camp, and I found a kettle, filled it with pease pottage which had been over a fire so long 'twas nearly as thick as the stuff in the crone's porringer, and sent Alfred to Couzeix with the meal. He returned, with the kettle, less than an hour later.

"Ain't there," he said.

"Did you seek her in some other place in the church?" I asked.

"Aye. Not much of a church. Wasn't behind the font or anywhere else. I even climbed the ladder to look in the tower."

I could not reprove Alfred for being lax in the search. The crone could barely walk, even aided with the crutch. She could surely not ascend to the tower, even as low and squat as it was, but Alfred had explored the space nevertheless. Perhaps the woman, fearing others might also discover her, had changed her refuge to one of the abandoned houses in the village, or set off alone for some nearby village where she might find succor, or was now wandering through the forest seeking her family. This troubled me. 'Twas my discovery of her hideaway which likely led to her fleeing the church.

"Odd, though," Alfred said. "That porringer was there, beside the font, and her crutch. There was yet a bit of pottage left in the bowl."

Why would the woman not take with her what little food she possessed, or consume it before she left the church? And how far could she travel without her crutch? Perhaps her family, suffering an attack of conscience, had returned to Couzeix for her. But why not take the porringer and crutch? The porringer was crude, to be sure, but even objects of little value have worth in a poor village.

While I considered this puzzle a page appeared with unwelcome news. Prince Edward wished my attendance upon him. Sir John had likely spoken to the prince.

Chapter 7

Prince Edward was not a happy man. The Cornish miners were not progressing as rapidly as he wished. When I approached the prince's tent a valet told me that his affliction had worsened. And now a suspicious death had been presented to him.

The prince had roused himself from his pallet and was seated upon an elaborately carved chair. If he was in discomfort he hid it well. His face showed more anger than pain. I suppose it is a kingly virtue, to remain enigmatic before one's subjects.

Then I considered that the scowl which shaped his brow was directed at me. A few days before he had thought me an honest surgeon. I hoped that when this interview was past he would yet do so. If he did not, I was in dire trouble.

I removed my cap, bowed deeply to the prince, and tried to assume an expression of curiosity and innocence. I am uncertain as to my success. I would be a poor player, I think, although it should have been easy for me to manage a blameless countenance, since blameless I was. I was not, however, curious. I knew why I had been called before the prince.

"Sir John Trillowe has lodged a charge against you," Prince Edward began. "Do you know of it?"

"Aye. He went first to Lord Gilbert, early this morn."

"What have you to say of the accusation?"

I explained briefly the unfortunate history I shared with Sir Simon, addressed the accusation, spoke of the moon, the cloudy night, and Lord Gilbert's admonition that I discover the cause of Sir Simon's death so as to vindicate myself. I then told the prince of traveling to Couzeix and finding the crone hunched behind the font, and concluded by telling him that the woman was apparently no longer in the church.

"There was blood upon the bucket?" Prince Edward said.

"Aye, but how it came to be there I cannot guess. It seems an odd weapon. The woman claimed to have heard no brawl in the night, when Sir Simon is thought to have been slain."

"Then why would he go to such a place alone?" the prince mused. "There to be slain by some enemy. Has any other man been found slain, or gone missing?"

"Nay... not that I've heard."

"So unless he traveled to that village alone, some other man must know how he came to be in that well."

"If he was taken there against his will," I said, "there may be several men who would know of the business."

"But you are not one of them, eh?"

"Nay, m'lord."

"Then why does Sir John accuse you?"

I explained about Kate and the burning of Galen House, which tale I had earlier omitted.

"Sir John said you had reason to hate his son. I see now he spoke true."

"'Twas Sir Simon who was filled with hate, m'lord. He lost a beautiful maid, he was required to pay ten pounds to replace my house, and his ear was misshapen, although I did my best to repair the injury."

"What injury?"

I was required to tell the prince of Sir Simon's fight in the streets of Oxford some years past and my work to sew his sliced ear back to his skull. Perhaps I became too precise in describing the difficulty of stitching an ear to its proper place.

The prince waved a hand and said, "Very well... I see. Wondered about the way he wore his cap."

As he spoke a valet entered the tent. Prince Edward looked from me to him and the fellow spoke.

"Lord Gilbert Talbot would speak to you, m'lord."

The prince looked to me with a quizzical expression. "Admit him," he said.

Perhaps Lord Gilbert had seen me follow a man wearing the prince's livery, or had been told that I was sent for. Whichever, he knew what my presence before Prince Edward likely meant.

Lord Gilbert entered the tent, removed his cap, and bowed.

He pretended surprise to see me there, but I knew 'twas a pretense. He carried the subterfuge well.

"Ah, Hugh, here you are. Have you learned more of Sir Simon's death? I am told you sought the place where he was found."

"Aye, m'lord. Couzeix is abandoned but for a crone I found hiding in the church. What happened there, whether Sir Simon was slain or fell into the well in a drunken stupor, I cannot say."

"Sir John accuses your surgeon of murder," Prince Edward said.

"Aye. He came to me early this morn with the charge. Nonsense. But if felony was done, Master Hugh will sniff it out. He has done me good service, seeking out malefactors."

"Sir John says that this fellow was seen, along with a groom of yours, with Sir Simon whilst he was yet alive."

"Sir Simon hated me," I said. "How likely is it that he would go off with me and another of Lord Gilbert's men in the dark of night?"

Prince Edward pulled at his beard. I was pleased to see that his frown had faded and had been replaced by an expression of puzzlement.

"Oh... aye, just so. I see. Found out malefactors, has he?" This to Lord Gilbert.

"He has. And if you grant him authority he will soon tell you if Sir Simon was slain, and if so, by whom."

"You will vouch for your surgeon? That he will be found here in the camp, and not flee."

"Aye," Lord Gilbert said.

"It may be necessary to return to Couzeix," I said, "or seek evidence in some other nearby places."

"Oh... hmm." The prince pulled again at his beard, then seemed to blanch, clutched at his gut with his left hand, and leaned forward in his chair.

For a moment I thought Prince Edward might topple from his seat, but the wave of pain passed, or he conquered it.

"Follow where the evidence leads," Prince Edward said through lips and teeth clenched tight in pain. "Lord Gilbert stands your surety?"

This last, voiced as a question, was spoken to my employer, who nodded and said, "I will do so."

The prince dismissed us with a wave of his hand – his right hand, for his left was yet gripping his belly. As I left the tent I saw a valet assist him from the chair, no doubt to lead him to a pallet where he might rest till the hurt in his gut passed. If it ever did.

"Where will you seek more knowledge of Sir Simon's death?" Lord Gilbert asked after we left Prince Edward's tent.

"I intend first to return to Couzeix."

"You believe there is more to learn there?"

"Mayhap. It is likely there would be much to learn amongst Sir John's men, but he will not permit me to ask anything of them, I think. So if I am to discover anything new of this matter, it will be in Couzeix."

"He wishes you guilty, even though you are not."

"Aye."

"Prince Edward has authority over Sir John," Lord Gilbert smiled. "If you believe it necessary to inquire of his men, the prince might be persuaded to exert his influence to make it so."

Lord Gilbert departed with Sir Walter Parmenter and Sir Henry Tawney to learn how the tunneling proceeded, all being hopeful that the Cornish miners would complete their work in another day or two.

I found Arthur and Alfred and told them we must return to Couzeix. They peered at me quizzically. Alfred perhaps assumed that I thought him incompetent. I explained:

"If you had done murder, and learned of an old woman who had sought refuge in the village church and who might know of your felony, what would you do?"

"Wouldn't take much to slay her," Arthur said. "Might just drop 'er in the well. 'Twas done once already."

"And did you ever wonder," I said, "how it was that Sir

Simon disappeared last night, and was found dead in that well this morn? And why a man would peer into a poisoned well seeking Sir Simon?"

"Someone in Sir John's camp knows somethin'," Arthur replied.

"Aye, and we must find the man and gain his knowledge. But first we will make haste to Couzeix. Mayhap if the woman was not pitched head first into the well, she may yet be alive, hiding somewhere other than the church. There was a tithe barn behind the priest's house, I remember."

I went first to the church to assure myself that the crone had not returned since Alfred had visited the place. She had not. 'Twas as Alfred had said – the crutch, cup, and porringer were hid behind the font, and no sign of the old woman.

Because of the shed erected over the well, little light was reflected from the surface of the water, so when I gazed into its depths I did not expect to see much of a reflection, and did not. I called into the well, trusting that if the crone was there and alive, she might respond.

No cry for help came from the well, but I thought I heard something, such as a person shifting their position. I looked to Arthur and Alfred for confirmation that some sound had come from the well in response to my words.

"Somethin's in the well," Alfred said, his ears being better than Arthur's.

"Could be a rat," Arthur said, "feastin' on whatever was tossed in there."

Just then I heard a faint splash from the depths of the well. Alfred heard it also. "Don't think rats dive into wells," he said.

I spoke again into the well, asking for some reply if a soul in the abyss could respond. Again no words came, but another faint scuffling was heard.

The bucket lay, with its hempen rope, where we had left it a few hours earlier. I picked it up and Arthur spoke.

"If someone's down there an' too weak to speak, they won't 'ave strength to hang on to that bucket whilst we haul 'em up."

"Not what I intend," I said. "You and Alfred must lower me into the well. I'll have a foot in the bucket."

"I'll go," Arthur said.

"Nay. You may be too fleshy for the rope. 'Tis worn. And you'll be needed here, with Alfred, to haul me up. Me and the old woman, if she is down there."

The well had no wheel or crank, so the hempen rope had been tossed over the top of the well many times. Its fibers had frayed against the stones. I worried that it might not hold my weight, but if the old woman was in the well, she was yet living and moving about in response to my calls. How much longer could she survive, injured and plunged into cold water? Likely not long enough to last while Alfred went back to camp for a sturdier rope.

The stone lining of the well extended above ground barely to my knee. I sat upon it, feet dangling into the opening. I told Arthur and Alfred to keep a firm grip on the rope, then placed a foot in the bucket – which, unlike most objects in Couzeix, was well made and reasonably new – and told them to lower me into the well.

I kept one hand upon the rope and pushed away from the side of the well with the other. All the while I peered into the gloom beneath my feet and called encouragement to whoso might be under me.

For a fleeting moment I thought it likely that I had embarked upon a fool's errand. But no, someone, or some thing, had moved in the depths of this well when I spoke into the opening.

My eyes became accustomed to the shadowy depths of the well and I realized that I must be near to the bottom.

"Easy, now," I shouted to Arthur, whose head and shoulders darkened the circle of light above me.

The crone's wimple was once white, I suppose, and had it been yet I might have seen it sooner – perhaps even from the top of the well. As it was, I saw it dimly in the shadowy light when the bucket and my foot were no more than an arm's length above the woman's head.

I pushed myself and the bucket from the side of the well just in time to prevent the bucket striking the old woman upon her head. She sat in water near to her shoulders. Her eyes stared blankly past me, open but unseeing. Beside her I saw the floating, bloated corpse of some furred creature – a goat, perhaps – which had been cast in to poison the water.

Had this been May rather than September the woman would likely have drowned, but a dry summer had decreased the water level in the well. I stepped from the bucket into water little more than waist deep.

The crone could not assist me in extricating her from the well. But would the hempen rope support the two of us as Arthur and Alfred drew us to the surface?

"What've you found?" Arthur shouted. "Rats, or the woman?"

"No rats," I replied.

"She alive? Can you fetch 'er out?"

"Alive, yes, but perhaps not for long. I'll fasten her to the rope, and tell you when to haul her up."

The knot fastening rope to bail was wet and difficult to undo. But when it was loosened I shouted to Arthur to slacken the rope, then ran it about the old woman's torso under her arms and knotted it in place.

"Haul away – but slowly," I said to Arthur's shadow in the circle of light at the well's opening. Immediately I felt the rope grow taut. The woman groaned as the rope cut into her flesh. I would have spared her this discomfort, but could think of no other way to get her out of the well quickly.

"Got 'er," I heard Arthur say, and saw the circle of daylight above me blocked for a moment.

"Rope's comin' back down," Arthur said, and a moment later it splashed beside me. I retied the line to the bail, once again placed a foot in the bucket, and shouted for Arthur to haul away. He did so with such enthusiasm I feared that the rope might part. It held, and some moments later I crawled, dripping, over the wall of the well and stood looking down upon a frail, unmoving form.

"Run to the camp," I said to Alfred, "and return with a litter. Make haste."

He did, and as he trotted away I bent to peer into the crone's face and spoke. "Who put you into the well?" I asked her in French. "Or did you tumble by mischance?"

The woman's eyes had been closed, but when I spoke they opened and finally seemed to focus upon me.

"Hurts," she whispered.

"What hurts?" Foolish question. After being dumped into a well she likely hurt everywhere.

"Me leg," she said, and glanced toward her right foot.

I saw then why the woman was in pain. Her ankle was broken, the foot jutting at an abnormal angle from her lower leg. The drop into the well, I thought, had done this.

"I have physics which will dull your hurt," I said. "But how did you come to be in the well?"

She was silent. Perhaps, I thought, she had swooned from the pain.

"*Trois*," she finally whispered. "Three." Try as I might, I could learn no more from her. She did not speak again.

Alfred and Uctred appeared carrying a litter. The woman remained senseless as we lifted her upon it, which was good, elsewise her broken ankle would have given her much pain. Half an hour later I opened the flap to my tent and Alfred and Uctred set the crone down gently. She was yet insensible, which condition I used to advantage, and went immediately to work straightening her broken ankle.

This was a waste. I had no sooner got the twisted ankle straight than the old woman heaved a sigh, as if some great weight had been lifted from her soul, and was still. I bent over her face, and pressed a finger to her neck. I felt no breath, nor could I find a pulse. Several hours in a cold well with a broken ankle had been too much for her aged body to endure.

Arthur had been peering over my shoulder as I straightened the woman's ankle. "Gone," he said. "Wonder what she meant when she said 'Three'?"

"Perhaps three men put her into the well. If so, they will likely be the same fellows who dropped Sir Simon into it. Why else would a well come to mind as a place to be rid of her but that it had been already used for the same purpose?"

"Aye... but not very successfully," Arthur said.

"That also puzzles me. Sir Simon was last seen just after sunset last night, so some man says, and was found in the well this morning but a few hours later... as if some man knew where to search for him. Sir John said he was seen in company with two others, which he claimed were you and me. We know that to be false. Perhaps the number is false also. Mayhap he was seen with three men."

"Wonder where it was Sir Simon was seen – if he was, an' the informer speaks true – an' where 'e was goin'?"

"Was he on his way to Couzeix, I wonder," I said. "And if so, why? There was nothing left in the village to attract him."

"Nothin' we know of," Arthur replied. Here was a new thought. "An' was 'e really with others, who seemed like us in the dark? Too great a riddle for me," Arthur concluded and scratched his head.

"She sought refuge in the church," I said. "Now she shall have it in the churchyard, till the Lord Christ returns."

I left my tent and sought Father Bartram. Lord Gilbert was prepared for any unfavorable contingency, having both surgeon and priest in his retinue. The woman must be shriven, and besides, since one corpse had already been laid to my charge, I did not want another to be added. I briefly explained my need, and the priest readily followed me back to my tent and the dead woman.

After last rites there was nothing more to be done for the crone. I arranged with Father Bartram to bury the woman next morn. But what to do with the corpse until dawn? It was not fitting that she should be placed outside the tent overnight, and to do so would surely invite unfavorable comment from those who passed by. So I spent the night with a corpse and with Arthur's snores. I did not sleep well.

73

We had no shroud in which to bury the woman. I thought that perhaps some cloth might remain in the church so sent Arthur to search the place. He returned empty-handed. Only a worn curtain across the Easter Sepulcher was there, he said, and he would not tear down such a sacred object for use as a burial shroud. The church had been stripped of everything else of slightest value. By whom, I wondered; Couzeix's villagers, or pillaging bands from French or English armies?

The lych gate to Couzeix's churchyard was decayed and near to collapse. Alfred and Uctred set litter and corpse upon the soil under the gate whilst Father Bartram folded his hands and prayed over the body. He spoke the words of Extreme Unction over the crone's waxen face, anointed her with oil from his chrismatory, then stepped aside as Uctred and Alfred lifted the litter and followed me into the churchyard.

Father Bartram sprinkled holy water upon a likely place, and with Arthur, Uctred, and Alfred taking turns at the spade we soon had a grave open to receive the old woman. Arthur struck another corpse just as I was about to tell him that the grave was deep enough, so she will have a companion, or likely several, to bide with her till judgment day.

While Alfred, Arthur, and Uctred plied the spade, I considered how it could have been that the old woman was discovered in the church. Did some other man seek knowledge of Sir Simon's death? Or did men – three, if that was what the crone meant by the word – search the church for anything of value which had not been hidden away or already stolen, and discover her rather than silver candlesticks?

In anger at being forestalled, such louts might pitch an old woman into a well for sport. That she would be found in the same place where Sir Simon was found but a few hours earlier would be a great coincidence. Bailiffs do not believe in coincidence.

Another thought came to me. Perhaps we were followed when we first came to Couzeix. Or men lurking in the village saw us enter the church. We were within the building longer than would be necessary to see that it was stripped of anything valuable. Such men, when we departed the church, might have entered the place to learn why we were detained. If they were the same knaves who slew Sir Simon, they might have considered the crone a witness to their felony and chosen the well as a place to silence her.

Did such men believe that I had already questioned her? Did she tell them so? Was she now lowered into her grave because I was too witless to look about me that morning to learn if we were followed as we walked to Couzeix, or so trusting of my sense that the village was abandoned that I was not alert to others watching when I entered or quit the church?

Whilst these thoughts passed through my troubled mind Father Bartram spoke the final collect for forgiveness, and Alfred set to work filling the grave.

The old woman could not have lived much longer. All men and women must die. But that is no reason to hasten the event.

If two murders had been done in Couzeix, I could see then no way to discover within the village who were the felons or why the murders were done. I could guess, but I have learned that doing so may mislead a man. He becomes convinced of his conjecture and seeks only evidence which will confirm it.

I thought it probable that the felons I sought would be found in the English camp, not within, or even near to Couzeix. What men of England disliked Sir Simon enough to slay him? A man's reputation may travel farther than he does, and Sir Simon's was not so laudable as he might have wished. Many knights are disagreeable fellows, yet no man seeks to slay them.

A few days past Sir Simon had made enemies of some of Sir Henry Morley's men. Would a man cheated at dice slay the man who had defrauded him? Some might. I decided to visit Sir Henry's tents and ask how much Sir Simon had gained from his deceit.

Chapter 8

Pottage to break our fast, pottage for dinner, more pottage for supper. The only variety was that some was of peas, some of barley. A loaf and roasted meat would have been worth much, but such fare was not for the likes of archers, men-at-arms, and bailiffs. Nor even for surgeons.

What was most lamentable about my diet was that Prince John of Gaunt and his knights were encamped but a hundred or so paces to the west of we of Lord Gilbert's company. Each morning but for fast days his cooks set flesh to roasting, and the breeze carried the scent to us as we ladled our meal from a common pot. A man will not linger long over a bowl of barley pottage to savor its goodness. I swallowed the glutinous meal, motioned to Arthur to follow, and set off through the sea of tents for Sir Henry Morley's camp.

I saw a familiar face as I approached Sir Henry's tents. Sir Charles de Burgh stood before Sir Henry's pavilion in conversation with several others. Sir Charles is Lord Gilbert's brother-in-law, having wed the beauteous Joan, Lord Gilbert's sister. I had heard that he has a son of Lady Joan.

I had seen the knight once a few weeks before, on the road from Calais, when he called upon his brother-in-law. His appearance had changed since I last saw him some years past. When we first met he was clean-shaven, as many young men, but now wore a beard which, like my own, betrayed his departed youth with a few gray whiskers.

When I first met Sir Charles he had seemed to me an upright knight, honest in dealings with other men. I thought he might be a source of information of the brawl between Sir Simon and those of Sir Henry's band. Perhaps he even took part in it.

Sir Charles saw me approach and recognized me. "Ah... Master Hugh. I give you good day." He stepped away from his companions and approached me. "How may I serve you?"

"How does Lady Joan?" I began.

"She is well. I pray. She is with child, our second. I trust this business will be soon over and done with so that I may return to Banbury."

"Does her wrist trouble her?"

Lady Joan, before she met Sir Charles, had been hunting with her brother and others whilst at Goodrich Castle, and was thrown from her horse when the beast refused a jump. Her wrist was broken in the fall, and I was sent for to deal with the injury. The fracture was grave, bone protruding from torn flesh and skin. When I first saw the injury I feared Lady Joan might lose her hand, amputation being required to prevent the wasting of the flesh, which calamity would spread to her arm and eventually take her life was the hand not removed. Such an amputation may also lead to death. I was much relieved when the fracture knitted well and the toxin faded.

"Rarely," Sir Charles said. "Occasionally on cold, damp winter days she suffers from an ache."

"Will you walk with me?" I asked Sir Charles. I preferred that his friends not hear my questions nor his answers. When we had gone twenty or so paces from his companions I spoke.

"Before we departed Bordeaux some of Sir Henry's men quarreled with Sir Simon Trillowe. Some dispute about dicing, I have heard."

"Dispute?" Sir Charles laughed. "You might call it that. A few bloodied noses and bruised heads. Good training for what may come. Is this about Sir Simon's death?"

"Aye. You've heard?"

"'Tis all through the camp. Hell itself will be defiled when Sir Simon arrives there. Tumbled into a well and drowned, some say. Drunk, perhaps. Others say an enemy may have slain him."

"Is this enemy named?"

"Aye." Sir Charles hesitated. "You are suspect. Do you know that this felony, if it so be, is spoken against you?"

"I do. Sir John went to Lord Gilbert and Prince Edward to denounce me."

"Yet you walk free. They do not believe the accusation?"

"Nay. I gave them good reasons to doubt it. But now I am assigned to discover what did happen to Sir Simon – mischance or murder."

"What have you learned?"

"Very little, but murder seems likely."

"And so you have come to Sir Henry's tents to seek those who brawled with Sir Simon and whoso was cheated at dice."

"Aye. Do you know the men?"

"I do. I am one of them. Not one of those cheated. I have given up dicing and gambling at Lady Joan's request."

Lady Joan's plea could make most men give up any vice.

"But when I saw two of my squires were set upon I joined the fray. 'Twasn't much of a fight. Sir Simon's men seemed unwilling to support him, knowing he was in the wrong. We vanquished the lot of them without having to draw a blade," he grinned.

"Were your knuckles sore after?"

Sir Charles looked to the back of his right hand. "No lasting injury," he said.

"Did Sir Simon return his gains?"

"Nay. Fled whilst the scrap was at its height, so I'm told. I was too engaged at the time to notice. Left his squires and grooms to defend his honor – a futile task – whilst he absconded with his booty. We've gained little plunder from the French since we set out from Calais, so Sir Simon decided to enrich himself by cheating his companions."

"How much was lost before his knavery was found out?"

"Four and six, so I was told."

Would a man slay another for four shillings and sixpence stolen from him? Men have done murder for less, I think.

"The greatest loss was to Edwin, my squire. You wish to speak to him of it? I'm certain he would not slay a man, but you will want to assure yourself of that rather than rely upon my word."

Sir Charles turned, motioned for me and Arthur to follow, and returned to the group of men with whom he had been in conversation when I first encountered him.

"Edwin," he said. "Here is Master Hugh de Singleton, bailiff to Lord Gilbert Talbot at Bampton. He wishes some words with you."

A dark-haired, slender youth of perhaps eighteen years looked to me. The lad was likely upon his first campaign, for he seemed callow at first glance. And at second glance. Edwin was some years from being fully grown. He stood no taller than my shoulder and could have weighed little more than eight stone. If he slew Sir Simon to avenge his loss he would, I thought, have required assistance, for Sir Simon was not a small man.

"W-what is it you wish of me?" the youth stammered.

"You lost at dice to Sir Simon Trillowe two weeks past?"

"Aye. Never knew a die could be weighted so as to fall as desired."

"Cunning men will use their wits to defraud the unwary," I replied.

The squire sucked upon his upper lip and nodded agreement. "I'll not be so duped again," he said.

"Sir Simon is dead, perhaps slain," I said.

I saw the lad's face fall and his eyes widen. Perhaps the implication of my words and my presence occurred to him.

"I heard of this yesterday," he said. "Fell into a well, drunk, men do say."

"Mayhap, but there is reason to suspect felony. Can any man vouch for your whereabouts Friday evening?"

"I can," another said. "Edwin was 'ere, playin' nine man morris by light of the fire till we sought our beds."

"You and he alone?"

"Nay. Ralph an' John an' Thomas was with us. Who else?" he said, scratching his balding head. "Oh, Osbert an' Walter was about."

Six men could vouch for the whereabouts of the swindled youth. Of course, some or all of them might have assisted Edwin in tipping Sir Simon into Couzeix's well. The lad was unlikely to have done such a thing alone. Asking of this would not produce an admission, so there was no point in doing so.

Edwin's face had gone white, and a nervous tick caused his

left eyelid to twitch. He wound his hands together before him as if washing some stain from them. This was not the behavior of a man with a clean conscience, I thought.

"When you left the camp yesterday afternoon," I asked the youth, "where did you go?"

I had no information that the lad had departed the camp, but thought that, if he had, I might catch him in a denial which could then be overturned. He seemed to reflect guilt for something. If he had witnesses to defend his presence in the camp when Sir Simon died, would he also find a defense for the time when the crone went into the well? "Three," the old woman had said. Edwin and two others?

My question struck a nerve. The lad looked as if I had thumped him between the eyes with a barrel stave. Oddly enough, his companions, including Sir Charles, turned to Edwin with some surprise, mouths open, as if my assertion was unanticipated. If it was, and Edwin had indeed slain the old woman, who had assisted the squire in seeking the crone and dropping her into the well? Perhaps he was strong enough to deal with her alone. She was frail, unlike Sir Simon.

My assertion that Edwin had left the camp at the time the old woman had been dropped into the well was an artifice, but it was clear to me from his response, and to the youth's companions as well, that he had absented himself from camp a day earlier.

Edwin's mouth opened and closed like a carp thrown upon the bank of a stream. "Who accompanied you," I said, "and where did you go?"

"N-n-no one."

"You went to Couzeix alone?" I said.

"Couzeix?" the lad said. "Where is Couzeix?"

There was sincerity in the question and his open-mouthed comportment, and I began to doubt the success of my gambit. Unless Edwin was a cunning player, he was genuinely ignorant of Couzeix.

"Not far from here," I said. "You and your companions could travel there and return in less than an hour."

"Couzeix's where Sir Simon was found," one of Sir Charles's companions said, glancing to Edwin. "So I heard."

"You heard?" I said. "Were you one who accompanied Edwin there?"

"Nay. Never been there; don't know where the place is. Never traveled from camp since we came before Limoges."

"This is true," Sir Charles said. "There are men of Sir Henry's band who are not lamenting Sir Simon's death, but so far as I know none has set off on his own... but for Edwin, perhaps."

He turned to Edwin and spoke. "Master Hugh would like to know, if 'twas not Couzeix where you went yesterday, where did you go?"

"I seen 'im goin' to the river," another of the group said.

The river was in the opposite direction from Couzeix. Of course, the lad might have walked away from the village to confuse any who might, like me, think he had to do with events there.

"Why go to the river?" I asked Edwin.

The squire blushed. Here was a strange response to a simple question.

"Why go to the river?" Sir Charles repeated my question. "Answer Master Hugh."

"W-w-went to bathe," he finally spluttered.

"Why so unwilling to say so?" I asked.

"Other lads do taunt me about it."

"What? That you wish to be clean and not stink?"

"Aye," Edwin said.

"You've gone to the river to bathe before?" Sir Charles asked.

"Aye... twice."

"And other lads do mock you for it?"

"Aye."

"Walk with me," Sir Charles said to me, and nodded toward an open space between tents. When we were out of earshot of his men and Arthur, he spoke.

"Edwin fears his own shadow. He has lived with me since

he was eight years old, his father desiring that he learn military arts from me, but he is not an apt pupil. You see how puny he is. I fear he will never make a soldier. A scholar, aye, but not a warrior."

"You think he would not have the pluck to attack Sir Simon? What if he had assistance? You think he went to the river, as he said?"

"Aye. He does not reek as most of us do. I should seek the river myself. Lady Joan will not welcome my return if I do not. Few men would follow Edwin to a fight. 'Twould be more likely he would follow others."

"Others who also lost to Sir Simon?" I said.

"Aye. Perhaps. Though none lost so much as Edwin, I think. Thomas lost a few pence, and also John."

"You saw the lad's face when I ventured the guess that he had been away from camp yesterday."

"Aye. Proves my point. Was he made of sterner stuff he'd not have recoiled so. And he'd not care if others teased him about cleaning himself in the river. He has not done mischief, I'd wager on it."

"Even after your promise to Lady Joan?" I smiled.

"Even then."

I did not offer to take Sir Charles's bet. Even after spending but a few minutes in Edwin's presence I was coming to agree with Sir Charles about the lad's character. He seemed unlikely to be capable of hate so strong that he could be compelled to do murder. But I've been wrong about such matters before. The Lord Christ has set limits to my wisdom, but none to my ignorance. This seems unfair. I resolved to keep Edwin in the brief list of potential felons I was building. Just in case.

Arthur and I bid Sir Charles "Good day", and returned to our own tents. If I had learned anything of value in visiting Sir Henry Morley's camp, I did not know what it might be.

Those who found Sir Simon's corpse in the well must be questioned, but I would not venture to Sir John's tents alone, or even with Arthur. A greater show of strength was required.

After a dinner of more pottage I gathered Arthur, Uctred, Alfred, and William, and we five set out for Sir John's tents. I told my companions to adopt a resolute expression, as if they had consumed a sour apple, and keep a hand resting upon the hilts of their daggers. Those who seem most ready for a brawl may be least likely to find themselves in one, and we five would be as welcome among Sir John's men as plague.

Sir John's tent was emblazoned with his arms and easy to identify amongst the others. We attracted much attention as we approached. When yet thirty or so paces off I saw a man glance in our direction, then enter Sir John's tent. So it was that he stood before me when I came to his tent. His jaw moved, and I caught the scent of roasted pork. I had interrupted his dinner. His victualer must have traveled far to find flesh for his master. I wondered in what other way I might offend Sir John.

"Why are you come hither?" he said. No polite greeting, but why did I expect one?

"I seek the same thing you seek," I said. "How did Sir Simon die, and was his death mischance or felony?"

"Bah... you know well 'twas felony. You are the felon."

This conversation had already attracted a crowd. Near twenty men had gathered, most appearing as determined as we. If Sir John wished it, we would be set upon and outnumbered four to one. I began to rue my decision to visit Sir John.

But the four men behind me wore Lord Gilbert Talbot's blue-and-black livery, and Lord Gilbert is a great baron of the realm. Sir John is but a knight. He would not be eager to provoke Lord Gilbert by attacking his bailiff and grooms. So I hoped.

"Spare me your accusation," I said. "'Tis all nonsense, as I think you well know. Who found Sir Simon in the well yesterday? Prince Edward wishes this business resolved, and has charged me to bring light to the matter. Those who found your son may be of some assistance."

I placed hands on hips, faced Sir John, and awaited his reply. I had mentioned the prince intentionally, perhaps adding more authority than Edward intended for me. But the result was exemplary. Sir John did not wish to annoy Lord Gilbert, and he surely did not want to offend Prince Edward with his intransigence.

"Osbert and John." Then, to one who stood close by, "Fetch them."

The fellow scurried away and soon returned with two well-dressed lads – squires, surely. I recognized one of the youths as Sir Simon's companion the night that he struck me at Leeds Castle, and the same who brought two shillings in exchange for Sir Simon's dagger. Sir Simon might be dead, but his influence lingered. Both wore their liripipes coiled low over one ear.

"This... fellow would speak to you of Sir Simon," Sir John said. He spat the word "fellow" as if it was a spoonful of hot pottage burning his tongue.

"You are Osbert and John?" I said.

"I'm John," one of the youths said. This the squire who had exchanged shillings for dagger. "He's Osbert."

"Come with me. We will walk a ways and speak of Sir Simon."

I saw the squires hesitate and look to Sir John. He frowned, but nodded toward me, indicating his permission. I turned to walk toward Lord Gilbert's tents, the lads fell in behind me, and behind them Arthur, Uctred, Alfred, and William. I wanted the squires well away from Sir John, his men, and their influence. And amongst Lord Gilbert's men their apprehension might loosen tongues.

I motioned to a bench before the cold embers of a fire pit and bid the lads sit. I remained standing. I have discovered in past interrogations that superior altitude is a good thing.

"Sir John said that you found Sir Simon in the well at Couzeix yesterday morn. At what hour?"

The lads looked to each other. Perhaps they sought some reason to dissemble. Apparently finding none, Osbert said, "Second hour."

"Why did you go to Couzeix, and why peer into a poisoned well?"

"At dawn yesterday, when Sir John learned that Sir Simon had not been in his bed all the night, he sent us, an' others, to seek him."

"Did Sir John, or any other man, send you to Couzeix?"

"Nay. We'd no instructions but to seek Sir Simon an' ask folk if they'd seen 'im."

"Had anyone... seen him, that is?"

"A man of Sir William Barnhill's troop said he saw him night before with two others, walkin' toward Couzeix. That's why we went there."

"Did Sir Simon tell you where he was going that night with two others? Did the fellow describe Sir Simon's companions?"

"Don't know where he was going. Sir William's man said one was tall an' slender, the other shorter and thick."

Here was the evidence Sir John apparently needed to accuse me of murder, if this squire spoke true.

He did not. How was I then to know?

"You told Sir John of this?"

"Aye. Then me an' Osbert went to Couzeix to see if Sir Simon was there... mayhap set upon in the night."

"Then what?"

"Found 'im in the well, didn't we?" Osbert said.

"Why look there?"

"Why not? He wasn't to be found in the houses, or church. We looked. Peered into the well as we passed by on our way back to camp."

"You found no other soul in the village?"

"Nay. All was gone. Not so much as a hen left behind. Saw a cat creep out of a barn. Nothing else alive there."

"The well is covered. How is it you saw Sir Simon at the bottom in early morning light?"

"Sir John didn't tell you?" Osbert said.

"Tell me what?" I replied.

"Wouldn't need to. If you are the man who did murder. He was nearly naked, white against the water, so when we looked into the well we saw some pale fellow was at the bottom."

"He was in the well head first, I was told."

"That's so."

"Did you then draw him from the well?"

"Nay. We shouted into the well, but there was no reply an' Sir Simon didn't so much as wiggle a toe, that we could see. Knew whoever was down there was dead. Not sure then 'twas Sir Simon, but who else could it have been? John ran back to tell Sir John an' I stayed to keep watch."

"Keep watch over a corpse?"

The lad shrugged a reply. "What else was I to do?"

"What else, indeed... Has Sir Simon been buried?"

"Tomorrow morning. Father Richard will say the mass. Laid out in a chapel, is Sir Simon. Sir John wished to take 'im back to East Hanney churchyard, but he'd stink long before that could happen... 'less Sir John could pickle 'im in a cask of wine."

"Sir Simon was a large man," I said.

"Aye," Osbert agreed. "Take a tun, an' a large one, to do so."

Whether or not Lord Gilbert's and Prince Edward's influence would sway Sir John to allow me to examine Sir Simon's corpse, I knew not. Nor could I imagine what I might discover if I did so. But it was sure that if I did not examine the dead man I would learn nothing, whereas an inspection might suggest whether or not the death was felony or mischance. Mischance? Why would a man, even drunk, stumble naked into a well? I sent John and Osbert back to Sir John with instructions that they must tell him that I would call upon him anon.

"You think them squires spoke true?" Arthur said when the lads were well away.

"If men have no reason to deceive they will usually speak the truth, I think," I said. "What is unclear is if they had reasons I do not know for speaking false. Anyway, I intend to call again upon Sir John."

"What d'you expect to learn from another visit to Sir John?"

"Very little. 'Tis Sir Simon I wish to visit. Perhaps he may tell me something his father and companions cannot."

"Or will not."

Chapter 9

Before questioning Osbert and John I had released Alfred, William, and Uctred. I sent Arthur to fetch them, desiring their presence when I again called upon Sir John Trillowe. Arthur did not soon return. He found William and Uctred, along with many others, watching the work of the Cornish miners to undermine the wall of Limoges. There was little to see. The shed of heavy planks protected the opening of the mine, so nothing of the excavation was visible.

French crossbowmen stood at the crenels, eager to send a bolt toward any man who ventured too close to the wall. Welsh longbowmen watched, but after loosing a few shafts in days past toward the French atop the town wall, had given up the sport as a waste of arrows.

The day after the shed was built the French dropped great stones upon its roof. One penetrated the planks with a splintering crash. So sawyers busied themselves at a pit and next night, when 'twas dark, another layer of planks was fixed atop the shed. Crossbowmen heard the work below them, and tried to interfere, but their shafts went astray in the night and I had no work to repair any wounds.

Soil and rock which the miners removed from under the wall could not be hauled away in the day. Those who did the work must leave the protection of the shed, but were near enough to the wall that a skilled crossbowman could put a bolt through a man or beast hauling a cartload of soil.

Arthur found Uctred and William shouting insults at crossbowmen who peered through the crenels. The Frenchmen returned the taunts, remarking, no doubt, upon the ancestry of the English soldiers. This exercise was futile, for the French understood few of the English barbs, and the English soldiers understood little French.

Alfred was not to be found, so we four returned to Sir John's tent, each one assuming a determined mien.

"Never," Sir John shouted when I told him that I wished to examine Sir Simon's corpse. "You have slain him. What more do you wish to do to him?"

"Reckon you'll need to call upon Prince Edward again," Arthur said.

Sir John looked from me to Arthur and back again. Sir John did not want me near Sir Simon's corpse. But neither did he wish to incur the prince's displeasure. If I reported to the prince that Sir John would not cooperate, the royal wrath might be unpredictable. Arthur sensed this, and knew that Sir John would also understand the possible threat. Arthur has wit as well as brawn.

I said no more, but stood squarely before Sir John and waited, as if I was certain that he would reconsider. He did.

"There's a chapel along that road," he said, turning to glance over his shoulder. "Father Richard is there, making ready the funeral mass. Tell him I grant you permission to... to examine my son."

It would be easy to dislike Sir John. Many men did. He had used his position as sheriff of Oxford for corrupt purposes, and had accused me unjustly of murder. But he had lost a son, and now had but two remaining to continue his line. How might I behave if I faced a man whom I believed had slain Bessie or Sybil?

"You must accompany me and tell him. The priest might not believe me, and I prefer that you witness my examination, so you will be sure that I did no malfeasance."

Perhaps Sir John would have preferred not to attend the inspection of Sir Simon's corpse so that he could then claim some cunning on my part if he did not agree with the result. Or perhaps he did not wish to look upon the remains of his son. I was not eager to do so myself, although I had many good reasons to be satisfied that Sir Simon now rested upon his bier. Uctred's blackened eyes were only now fading, his nose was yet sore and swollen, and in memory I could yet smell the ashes of the first Galen House.

The chapel was five hundred paces to the north of the camp, one of those shelters where pilgrims and travelers might seek refuge for a night and pray. Until this day I had not known of its existence, the chapel being away from the road which we used to approach Limoges, and beyond a hill and wood from the camp. A low stone wall covered in vines and shrubbery enclosed a chapel yard of perhaps thirty paces on each side. I saw two fresh graves there. Standing siege can be a deadly business, even before arrows fly and swords flash.

The chapel was of stones, crudely finished many centuries past, I believe, with a slate roof. The building was no more than six paces wide and eight deep, there were two windows, covered with oiled skins, on each side, to light the interior, and the door stood open. Four candles burned between bier and altar. I would have preferred to move Sir Simon out of the chapel, where better light might tell me more of his death, but thought that Sir John might object. This, however, proved unnecessary.

Sir Simon had been washed and lay covered with a black shroud. Where Sir John could have found such a winding cloth in the midst of a siege I know not.

I moved the candlestands to Sir Simon's head to provide as much light as possible and began my examination. I expected to find a lump or laceration upon the rear of his skull where some man had delivered a blow with a bucket.

Rigor mortis had faded long since, so I could easily turn Sir Simon's head. When I did so his misshapen ear was turned to me and I was reminded of my clumsy attempt to stitch the organ back to its proper place. Next time I will know better how to proceed.

I carefully inspected Sir Simon's skull. He had begun to go bald, emulating his father, which made the examination some easier. I found no lump or cut which might indicate where a blow had fallen. This did not surprise me greatly. If a man is slain by a blow to his head and dies immediately, often no swelling, or very little, will appear. I cannot tell why this is so.

But I found no wound, which did surprise me. I was

convinced that Sir Simon had been rendered unconscious, then dropped head first into the well, where he drowned. The blood upon the bucket seemed to make this a logical assumption. Perhaps the reddish stain upon the bucket was not blood. If it was, the blood did not come from the back of Sir Simon's skull, for there was no laceration there. I could not credit this, so examined the scalp again, with the same result.

Sir John had watched me carefully, and when I went the second time to the rear of Sir Simon's skull he said, "What have you found?"

"Nothing."

"You seem troubled. Why so?"

I told Sir John of the bucket at Couzeix's well, and what I assumed had taken place at the well. He listened with pursed lips. I believe he began to think me innocent of Sir Simon's death, if he had ever really thought me responsible. Perhaps, I thought, I may no longer fear the shadow of a noose above my head.

I peeled back the shroud from Sir Simon's upper body to seek some other wound or sign of injury. The bloodied bucket yet puzzled me. If Sir Simon was struck somewhere on his body below the neck by a bucket, even a blow which would tear open his skin and cause blood to flow, 'tis unlikely that he would have swooned and been rendered incapable of defending himself. And those who had prepared his body for burial would have seen such a wound and surely reported it to Sir John. So whence came the blood on the bucket? And was Sir Simon dead before he went head first into the well?

"Who of your men drew Sir Simon from the well?" I asked.

"Osbert and John were there, since it was they who found him. Three others."

"Fetch them. Before I seek other sign on Sir Simon's corpse I must ask of them a question. I don't need all five. Two or three will do."

Several of Sir John's men had followed us to the chapel. He sent one to do my bidding and urged the fellow to make haste. He did so, and John and an older man soon entered the chapel, peering about in the dim light as their eyes adjusted from the bright sunlight beyond the chapel door.

"Master Hugh has need of you," Sir John said by way of greeting. John and the other turned to me. I thought John seemed pale, but perhaps 'twas the dim light, or the presence of his friend's corpse.

"When you drew Sir Simon from the well, and when you carried him back to camp, did water issue from his mouth?"

The older man looked to the squire for a moment, then spoke. "I never seen any water. Did you?"

John shook his head. "Don't think so."

"Why do you ask?" Sir John said. "Why might this be important?"

"I'm not sure that it is," I said. "But if Sir Simon fell into the well by mischance, yet breathing, and there drowned, his lungs would fill with water. Some would leak from his lips, I think. If he was dead when pitched into the well, there would be no water within his lungs, for his breath would have already stopped."

"Ah," Sir John said. "I see."

If Sir Simon drowned in the well, I thought, and no water was seen issuing from his lips when he was lifted from its depths, then perhaps his lungs were yet filled and pressure applied to his chest might force some out. I explained the thought to Sir John so that he would not mistake what I was about to do.

"Hmmm. Well, do what you must."

I asked Arthur's help and together we turned Sir Simon so that he lay upon his stomach. I took a position before Sir Simon's waxen face, opened the lips, and told Arthur to press firmly upon Sir Simon's back. He did so. No liquid came from the opened mouth.

I told Arthur to press down again, more firmly this time. Few men could do so more forcefully. Arthur did as I requested, and so close was I to Sir Simon's mouth that I felt air flow from between his lips. I drew back from the stink of death. Air had come forth, but no water.

"What have you learned?" Sir John demanded.

"He did not die of drowning in the well, I think. He was dead before he went into it."

"You are certain of this?"

"Certain? Nay. Few things in life are certain."

"Then 'twas felony, and no mischance."

"Aye. Did those who found Sir Simon seek his clothes?"

Sir John shrugged. "Dunno... I didn't."

"You didn't wonder why he was found naked?"

"Wasn't naked, truly. Had on his kirtle and cotehardie. 'Twas only his chauces and braes that were gone. I wondered more at why he was found dead. What happened to his clothes seemed less important at the time. And I thought if Lord Gilbert searched your tent later, we'd find his apparel."

"You may search when you will. You'll find none of Sir Simon's garments in Lord Gilbert's camp."

"Not now, when you had opportunity to discard them."

Sir John was not so ready to give up his belief in my guilt as I had thought.

Arthur and I rolled the corpse to its back and I continued the search for a fatal wound. A few years past I had encountered a similar puzzle when a guest at Bampton Castle was found dead in his bed of a morning. 'Twas as much luck as wisdom which led me to the cause of the knight's death. A bodkin had been thrust through the man's ear, into his brain, whilst he slept. The wound was nearly imperceptible.

With this fresh in my mind I examined Sir Simon's ears, nose, mouth, even his navel, for any evidence that these had been pierced. There was none.

When Arthur and I had turned the corpse to its back, the arms we allowed to lie beside the corpse rather than across the breast with hands folded, as we had found Sir Simon upon his bier. This bier was narrow, so as I sought for some fatal wound, his left arm fell from the platform and dangled straight down. This seemed an undignified posture, even for the dead, and so I grasped the cold flesh to replace the limb upon the bier. As I did so a slight discoloration caught my eye.

The hair of Sir Simon's armpit nearly obscured this anomaly. Rather than place the arm across the chest, as had been, I lifted it vertical to see more clearly what mark was there.

'Twas a wound, nearly hidden in the foliage which sprouts in such a place. Why will a man become bald upon the top of his skull as he grows old, yet have the fur of a squirrel's tail under his arms till the day he dies?

I saw no blood. If there had been bleeding when the puncture was first made, immersion in the well had washed it away. The soaking had caused the skin about the cut to pucker, so that I could see that the wound was no insignificant scratch. The blade had not been slashed across Sir Simon's side. The cut was little longer than the width of my thumb, but deep. A dagger had evidently been thrust into Sir Simon's heart and lungs from under his arm.

Sir John watched my examination but from where he stood could not see what had caught my eye. But he saw that something was amiss.

"What is there?" he said. "What have you found?"

I motioned for him to come close, held Sir Simon's arm high, and said, "Look there." Sir John did so.

"What is there? What is that mark?"

Because the chapel had but four skin-covered windows, and there were few candles, a close inspection had been necessary to identify the wound as made by a dagger. I moved a candlestand near and told Sir John to look closely. A man who has seen battle has seen wounds made by daggers thrust into a man. Sir John knew well what he then saw.

"Slain," he said.

"Aye. So I believe," I replied.

"But, if not you, whoso hated my son as to do murder?"

"You would know better than I," I said. "I wished to have as little to do with him as possible. Who were his friends? Who was he likely to go off with in the night?"

"A friend would not slay him."

"Friends may have quarrels, and do things in heat that they later rue."

Sir John did not respond to that assertion. Perhaps he was considering which of Sir Simon's friends might have had a falling out with him. I spoke again.

"Where are his chauces and braes? And his dagger? If they are found we might learn something from them of this felony. And was there no cut in his cotehardie to mark the place where he was stabbed?"

"I saw a seam opened, so I thought, under the arm of his cotehardie. But there was no bloodstain there. Mayhap water from the well washed the blood away. And no point in seeking his garments in his tent," Sir John said. "He'd not go off half naked."

"Aye. Unless the murderer took clothing and dagger, perhaps to sell, the garb will be somewhere near to Couzeix, likely hidden."

"Will you seek it?" Sir John asked.

"Aye. This day. I and my men will go to Couzeix. Some of your lads might come also. The more searchers, the greater chance of discovery. If there is anything left in Couzeix to discover."

There was.

To assist me in searching Couzeix, Sir John sent John the squire and the older groom who had helped fish Sir Simon out of the well. With Arthur, Uctred, and William we were six searchers. If we could not find Sir Simon's clothing in Couzeix, it was not likely to be found anywhere. John did not seem pleased to be assigned this work. He had already found a corpse. Perhaps he thought that his obligation in the matter of Sir Simon's death had been discharged.

At Couzeix I assigned each of the searchers two houses and their accompanying sheds and barns. I walked to the end of the village where a more substantial house abutted the churchyard. This, I thought, was likely the vicarage.

Nothing of value remained in the house. The priest had fled the village with his parishioners, taking with him all that he possessed. Behind the vicarage was the village's small tithe barn. A large, crude iron lock was fixed to a hasp which in turn fastened an iron bar across the door.

I tugged at the bar and felt it move. Several iron nails driven through a hinge secured the bar to the hinged side of the door, and these were loose due to the age and desiccation of the jamb. I pulled vigorously upon the bar and it came free in my hand. I wondered that no man before me had done the same.

Three slit-like, skin-covered windows, purposely made too narrow for a man to slip through, gave some light to the interior of the barn. I saw there three sacks, filled with grain and perhaps also peas and beans. Vermin had gnawed a hole at the base of one sack, and barley spilled out upon the packed earth of the floor.

I carefully examined the sacks, but found no sign that they had been recently moved. No garments were hidden under them. Two sacks, however, had been opened and peas and barley taken. When, I could not know. Perhaps the priest had taken from his store before he fled. If the village priest was as poor as his parish he would have no cart, nor beast with which to draw it. What grain he could not carry would need to be left behind, locked away, for the priest's return. The barn had no loft, so nothing could be hid in the rafters. I left the barn and entered the church.

The font was locked, of course, so witches could not get holy water for their black arts. The lock was heavy and had been greased with lard or some such stuff. There was no sign that any man had tried to pry the lock from its hasp or force open the lid of the font. And who would think to hide braes and chauces in a font?

I peered under and behind every object and table in the church. I even tested the altar. It was fixed firmly to the flags. The stubby tower rose over the west entrance to the church. A ladder gave access to the upper room of the tower. A bell hung there, but elsewise the small chamber was empty of all but cobwebs. I descended to the ground and walked slowly about the church once again. 'Twas then I noticed the threadbare curtain hung across the Easter Sepulcher. The drape was so old and faded it was not thought worth taking, either by the vicar or by pillagers. And who would risk the wrath of God by absconding with such a sacred object? I idly brushed the timeworn velvet aside, expecting to find nothing there of import. 'Twas the yellow cap which first caught my eye.

The cap, with its long liripipe, lay atop brown chauces, and beneath the chauces I found white linen braes, all of these garments carefully folded. Were these Sir Simon's? I remembered seeing him wear brown chauces, and his usual cap was yellow. Whose clothing would be cast off in such a hidden place but for a man who would no longer need the apparel?

A man in a hurry would not have placed the clothing so neatly. Why do so, I wondered, even if haste was not required?

I lifted the braes and then the chauces, seeking a cut or bloodstain on the fabric. I found nothing on either article. Were these not Sir Simon's dress? If not his, whose, and why would such be hid away in an Easter Sepulcher? If the garments were Sir Simon's, and I felt certain that they were, had they been removed before he was pierced? By whom? Did Sir Simon disrobe himself? If not, who had required that he do so? Discoveries in the matter of Sir Simon's death were raising as many questions as they answered.

I had found no dagger with the clothing. I remembered the weapon well. 'Twas finely made, and worth a shilling or two, but there was little distinctive about it. And no shoes were in the Easter Sepulcher. One dagger is much like another; likewise shoes. A felon could carry these off and use or sell them with no one the wiser.

I took the garments and departed the church through the tiny porch. I had told my companions to meet at the well when they had completed searching their assigned places. Uctred and John were there, empty-handed, which, after my discovery in the Easter Sepulcher, was no surprise. John saw me leave the church, spoke, and Uctred turned. Together they gazed at the bundle in my arms and the squire backed away.

"Are these Sir Simon's chauces and cap?" I asked John.

"Aye. You'd see yellow caps like his, but not of that pale hue. Not in the camp, anyway."

Within minutes Arthur, William, and Sir John's older groom had completed their searches and joined us at the well. No one had seen shoes or dagger. William had discovered an old, discarded, moth-eaten tunic, but Sir Simon would not have owned or worn such apparel.

"Odd, though," William said. "Tunic wasn't in a house. 'Twas in a barn, tossed in a corner."

We were on our way from the village when William's discovery caused me to hesitate.

"Where is the barn where you found the cast-off tunic?" I said.

"Just there," he pointed, "behind second house."

"We will see what is there," I said, although at the time I had no notion that a worn tunic could have anything to do with Sir Simon's death.

William led the way through the overgrown toft to the ramshackle structure. Several chinks in the daub allowed air, light, and vermin into the barn, and the thatching was rotted and thin.

The door stood open, and William stood aside from it so that I could enter. Holes in walls and roof allowed enough light that the dark fabric was visible upon the lighter straw.

"Is this where you found it?" I asked William as we gazed upon the tattered garment.

"Nay. 'Twas in the corner, just there, as if 'twas thrown there."

The tunic was surely ancient. 'Twas nearly threadbare and worn through in several places, and the hems at neck, sleeves, and the base of the tunic were frayed.

I lifted the tunic for a closer examination. It was worth little, but to an impoverished villager even such shabby garb would have some value. Why was it left behind when the householder fled?

And why the straw? There was no sign that any beast had made the barn a home. No manure littered the pounded earth of the floor. The straw covering a part of the floor seemed fresh, cut this year after the harvest, perhaps only a few weeks ago. With holes in the roof and walls of the barn, straw would soon become wet and moldy. Why would a man scatter fresh-cut straw if he knew he was to abandon his place to seek safety elsewhere?

I am unsure if my curiosity is due to my service to Lord Gilbert, or to a natural nosiness. But I was not satisfied with any explanations for the tunic and the fresh straw which came to me. I lifted the tunic from the straw, took it to the toft, and in the sunlight laid it upon the earth.

"What you searchin' for?" Arthur asked.

"Don't know," I shrugged. "Does it not seem odd that this ragged tunic should be found in a decrepit barn with a layer of fresh straw nearby?"

Arthur pulled upon his beard and considered my words whilst I knelt in the dirt to examine the tattered wool. Whoso had previously worn the tunic had dark hair. Close examination yielded three long brown strands. I held them up to the light. These did not come from Sir Simon's pate, I thought. He was fair, nearly blond, whereas these hairs were near to black. And each was as long as my forearm. Here were hairs from a woman's scalp.

I had found the hairs near to the opening for the neck, so their location made sense. But the length of the tunic did not. I stood and held the garment to me. It fell to just above my knees. Here was a man's tunic with three strands of some woman's hair upon it.

Perhaps the hair came from a child, a lass, who often wore her father's worn tunic. This was surely possible, but did not explain why it was left behind when the family fled.

I was yet holding the tunic to myself, pondering these things, when Arthur said, "What is there?" and pointed to the garment.

Because of the brown color of the tunic I had not noticed the stain under the sleeve. 'Tis a wonder Arthur saw it, and he might not have but that the tunic was so old and faded that a deeper color was noticeable. Where the dark stain was the tunic

98

was stiff. Had blood made this stain? I lifted the tunic for a closer examination, thinking I might see under the sleeve a slash made by a dagger thrust.

Not so. The garment was whole. And because dried blood is brown, as was the tunic, there was no way to know certainly that the blot was blood.

First blood on the rim of a bucket, now blood, perhaps, upon a frayed tunic. Or was my imagination seeing bloodstains where none were? Surely Sir Simon would not have worn such a tunic, and when he was pierced he was surely not wearing the garment. For what purposes does a man disrobe?

To sleep? But why in Couzeix? Surely he would not slumber upon the flags of the church, nor would he seek a decaying barn for his rest.

A lass, then? Could it be that he caught some maid returning to her village and forced himself upon her? Or did she meet him willingly? Perhaps for a few silver coins. Couzeix was clearly a poor village.

But if Sir Simon went to Couzeix for a tryst, why did he die there? If 'twas a lass that brought him to Couzeix, did she have an enraged father? More questions, and few answers. I folded the frayed tunic and placed it under my arm, along with the clothing from the Easter Sepulcher, and set off for the English camp.

Sir John readily identified his son's garments when I laid them before him. "Where'd you find them?" he asked. "Were they where you left them?"

I told him where I had found the cap, chauces, and braes, ignoring his imputation, then brought the old tunic to his attention. Sir John fingered the threadbare wool, a curl of distaste upon his lips.

"Never seen that before. Even my villeins do not wear such ragged stuff."

"Did Sir Simon ever speak to you of seeking maids hereabouts?" I asked.

"Hah. My son was always seeking maids, here or elsewhere. Much like other young men."

"But he never said anything about finding a lass in Couzeix or meeting her there?"

"Nay. Wouldn't, would he? If he'd found a willing lass he'd keep the discovery for himself."

I began to think that Couzeix was not so vacant as I had thought. Folk might know of the grain in the decrepit tithe barn and might visit the place in the night. I had found a way to enter the barn; perhaps others had also done so. Two of the sacks stored within it had been opened.

Someone had scattered fresh straw upon the floor of a decaying barn. Before or after Couzeix's inhabitants fled?

I am a dolt. 'Twas while considering these things in my bed that night that I suddenly remembered what I had not seen in Couzeix's church when I found Sir Simon's clothes. The porringer and wooden cup which had sustained the crone were not in their place behind the font. I had not seen them elsewhere in the church, either. Someone had removed them and I was too intent upon other matters to notice. The porringer and cup were worth little, but to an impoverished villein they would be too valuable to discard.

Arthur was already snoring upon his cot when the missing porringer and cup occurred to me. 'Tis always best to fall to sleep before Arthur does, as his snoring will prevent Morpheus from attending any man within twenty paces of his slumbering form. So 'twas likely past midnight when I finally fell to sleep. In the wakeful hours of the night I devised a plan whereby to discover if Couzeix was visited more often than I had supposed. But the scheme, as any other, would best be effected after a night of sound sleep.

I awoke before dawn, which, now that days were growing shorter, was easy to do. Arthur grunted with displeasure when I prodded him awake, but as I explained the reason for drawing him from slumber he became eager to see what might be the result of my plan.

Chapter 10

We swallowed cold pease pottage, washed the meal down with watered ale, then set off on the darkened road to Couzeix. The eastern sky was growing yellow with the dawn, and I wished to be in the village and hid before the sun appeared. We made haste.

The house which included a cistern was in such a place in the village that from its skin-covered windows a man could see to nearly every corner of Couzeix, if he peeled the skin away from a corner of a window.

Which is what I did. Arthur and I had crept as soundlessly as possible into Couzeix, gone to the rear of the house, and pushed through a rear window to enter the place. 'Twas black as Lucifer's heart, but the skin windows at the front of the house glowed softly in the pale light of early dawn.

I sent Arthur to one window with instructions to peel back a corner of skin, just enough that he could see through. I did the same with a second window. A crude table and benches had been left when the family fled, likely because they had no cart with which to transport them. We moved the benches to the windows and sat peering through the tiny gaps we had made.

Two hours later full daylight illuminated the empty street and vacant houses of Couzeix. Would a man enter the village when he might be seen? Should we have come to the place earlier, or waited till dark? 'Twas now too late for second thoughts. Arthur and I were hidden in Couzeix and there we might as well remain.

Near to midday I saw the cat. It ran from behind the vicarage and darted behind a barn opposite the house which hid Arthur and me. Arthur also saw it run.

The cat was not prowling for vermin. A cat will run only to catch something or to escape from some other thing. I could see no prey where the cat disappeared. Perhaps something frightened the animal behind the vicarage. Or some person.

The tithe barn was not visible behind the vicarage, being quite small and my vantage point not the best. I kept my eyes upon the space between church and vicarage from whence the cat had come, to see what, or who, might have frightened the scrawny feline. Had it been seeking its dinner amongst the vermin I knew inhabited the tithe barn, and been chased off by someone also seeking a meal from the vicar's store?

I had nearly given up the thought when I saw a head appear around a corner of the vicarage. Slowly, after studying the village to be certain that no man saw her, a lass appeared. She wore a ragged blue cotehardie and carried a small sack – filled with the vicar's corn, no doubt. Her tangled hair was long and dark.

"You see 'er?" Arthur whispered.

"Aye."

"Shall we seize 'er?"

"Not yet. Watch where she goes."

The lass crept from church to house, trying to blend with walls and shadows, till she came to the house behind which we had found the tattered tunic in a barn filled with fresh straw. She followed the shadowed wall to the rear of the house, disappeared, then a moment later reappeared. She cast her eyes about as if seeking some person or thing, and I thought I knew what that thing was. She sought the ragged tunic which had been tossed to a corner of the barn. Ragged it was, but not much more tattered than the cotehardie she wore. Why would she know where the tunic had been? The time had come to ask her.

I motioned for Arthur to leave his window and come near. I told him that we would leave the house through the rear, as we had entered it, go in opposite directions around the place, and come upon the lass from two ways. If she fled from one of us she would run toward the other.

Arthur has many fine qualities, but agility is not one of them. The lass saw us approach, decided that I was closest and therefore the greater threat, and turned to run past Arthur. She did so, avoiding his ponderous gait with ease. He turned to follow after as she danced past, but he might as well have been a bear attempting to catch a hind. If the lass was to be caught and questioned before she reached the wood and disappeared, it would be up to me.

Fear gave wings to the maid's heels. We were a hundred paces beyond the church before I caught her. She had refused to release the sack of grain, or she might have made good her escape. Kate's cookery has slowed my pace, I fear.

I seized the lass by her collar and spoke reassuringly to her that I meant her no harm. This had no effect. She shook so violently that I thought she might swoon. Her agitation, I believe, was not due to exertion, but to fear.

I spoke to the lass in French, but her reply, when she was finally able to speak, was in the same dialect the crone in the church had used, and I could make little of her gasping words. I took the sack of rye in one hand, grasped a wrist firmly enough with the other that she could not flee, and led her back to the village.

The church porch, I thought, would be a convenient place to speak to the lass of recent events in Couzeix, and Arthur, not of much value in a chase, would serve well to impede an escape if the maid thought to flee through the porch entrance.

Stone benches occupied both sides of the tiny porch. I pointed the lass to one of these, told Arthur to block the entrance, and sat opposite the maid.

When she understood that I seemed to have no evil intent upon her, her quaking ceased, and after much repetition I learned her story.

Her name was Heloise. She came to the village nearly every day to get food from the tithe barn, which a small person could enter from the rear through a place where the wattles and daub were rotten.

The crone hiding in the church was her grandmother, and she knew not what had become of her until I told her of the fresh grave in the churchyard. A tear flowed down a grimy cheek at the news.

Her mother and younger sister, she said, were hid in the

forest shelter two miles from Couzeix. There was no man there; her father and a brother were dead, and another brother was taken when the Duke of Berry captured Limoges and compelled him to serve in his army.

Each day when the lass returned to her village she had brought pottage for her grandmother and filled her small sack with barley or rye or peas to take back to her mother and sister.

"What will become of them," she wailed, "if I am hanged for theft?"

I tried to reassure the lass that I had no authority over her, nor would I turn her over to one who did. Such reassurance was difficult enough for me to explain in Parisian French. I am yet unsure that the maid completely understood my words.

When I asked of the tunic found in the barn the lass fell silent. Her reluctance to speak was not due to ignorance of the garment, I felt sure, but to knowledge she did not wish to share.

Folk who are asked questions they find inconvenient will avoid their interrogator's eyes, I have found, and cast their gaze about as if seeking a deceptive but credible reply, or a way of escape. Heloise did this; glanced to Arthur where he stood squarely in the porch entrance, decided that flight was impossible, and so began to dissemble.

The tunic was her brother's, she claimed. He had no need of it, being given the Duke of Berry's livery when taken into his service. When Heloise discovered that it had been left behind, she said, she washed it with water from the bailiff's cistern and spread it upon the fresh straw to dry, intending to return for the garment soon.

"You washed it?" I asked.

The lass nodded.

"Then why was a bloodstain found under the arm?"

Heloise swallowed deeply. This was a reply of sorts, but not the one she intended.

"Was your brother attacked whilst he wore the tunic? Did the Duke's men wound him when he was taken?"

The maid nodded. "Aye... that's how it was."

"But you washed the garment, you said. Why does the blood from your brother's wound remain?"

Heloise again fell silent, caught out in deception.

"You went daily, or near so, to the church to take food to your grandmother, so you said."

"Aye." The lass brightened, seemingly pleased to no longer be questioned about the tunic.

"Did you ever see any other folk about the church when you came to your grandmother? Perhaps men from the English army seeking candlestands or plate?"

"Nay," she shook her head. "Vicar took all such stuff with him when he fled."

"What of the Easter Sepulcher? Did you see who placed a man's clothing there?"

"Clothing?" she said. "In the Easter Sepulcher? Why would a man's garments be there?"

Heloise's words, what I could understand of them, spoke ignorance, but her reddened cheeks and hands twisting together said otherwise.

"Did you ever see three men together in Couzeix?"

"Nay. Never saw no one here. All are away."

"Not folk of the village. Men of the English army. Did you see me and my men when we first came to Couzeix a few days past?"

"Nay. Never stayed here long. Fed grandmother, fetched more corn, and left."

"Just so. Dangerous for a maid to be alone with an army of bored soldiers so nearby."

The lass's eyes fell to her hands, which were yet twisting upon her knees. She did not disagree with my assertion, and I wondered if she had reason to know its truth. I asked.

"You said that you never saw men in Couzeix when you came seeking food. But that is not true, is it? Did they do you harm? Is that why you will not speak of it? Or them?"

"Wasn't three," the lass finally whispered, "but two."

"Two men came upon you whilst you were in the village?"

"Aye. Found me in the church, with grandmother."

"They had their way with you?"

"Aye," Heloise sniffed. "Only but one. Sent the other away, he did. Gave me a silver coin and said that there'd be another did I meet him here on the morrow."

"Did you?"

"Aye," she said.

"You met a man here in Couzeix twice?"

"Nay... three times."

Was that what the crone meant when she gasped, "*Trois*"? Did she mean to say, "*Trois reprises*"?

"You met the man in the church?"

"Nay, but for the first time when he come upon me sudden."

"Where, then?"

"Barn, behind me house."

"Where the tunic was found. The tunic you claimed to have washed, but did not. Did the man give you a coin each time you met?"

"Not the third time."

"Why not? Did he tire of you so soon?"

The lass's lip began to quiver, and a tear sought a path down her cheek.

"Why not?" I asked again.

"He was slain," she finally whispered.

"The murdered man, had he a misshapen ear, standing from the side of his head?"

"Aye," Heloise whispered.

"What coins did he give you? Do you yet have them? I will not seize them."

The lass nodded and reached for a threadbare woolen pouch under her belt. She likely thought that I would take her money, regardless of my assurance, and had no fight left in her to object. With Arthur looking on, no wonder. She opened her hand to show two farthings. Sir Simon had valued the lass's favors no more than a quart of cheap ale.

"How was the man slain?" I asked.

"Not sure. I was upon the tunic, me eyes closed, an' it bein' near dark, when 'e rose up an' I heard 'im say, 'You… why are you come?' Next I knew, he groaned and fell upon me. All bloody he was, too. I didn't slay him," she added hurriedly.

Heloise bit her lip. Perhaps she feared that she had said too much.

"You lied about washing the tunic. Are you also lying now?"

"Nay, sir. Thought you being English, you might be a friend of the man what was slain, and think I slew him."

"No friend of ours," Arthur growled.

"Did the murdered man tell you his name?" I asked.

The lass shook her head.

"He was Sir Simon Trillowe. Do you know where he was found?"

She shook her head "No" again.

"Men found him next day, face down in yon well. He spoke to his attacker, you said?"

"Aye… said, 'You – why have you come here?'"

"Was there but one man, or several?"

"Dunno. Nearly dark, an' when he groaned an' fell upon me I was confused. And then I felt the blood."

"What did you then do?"

"Ran, didn't I. Thought if some man pierced 'im, they might do the same to me."

"You left Sir Simon upon the tunic and fled? Was he yet alive?"

"Dunno."

"When you fled the village, did you see others about? Did any man try to follow you as you fled?"

"Nay. All was quiet. Don't know where him as did murder went. I think he fled the barn as soon as he struck the man who gave me the coins."

A frightened lass running through the near darkness might not notice other folk about Couzeix, even if there had been. Heloise had not at first wanted to tell me of events in the village, but had evidently come to trust me and so told me of Sir Simon's death.

None of her menfolk had come upon the two of them and

107

sought vengeance against Sir Simon, for they were dead or away. And Sir Simon had recognized his attacker, even in the dim light of dusk.

"How is it that Sir Simon's clothes were placed in the Easter Sepulcher?" I asked.

"Came back next morn, at dawn, to see was he dead or alive. He was gone, but his braes and chauces were yet in the barn. Didn't think he'd leave without them. Knew then 'e was dead."

"So you folded his clothes and hid them in the church, in the Easter Sepulcher," I concluded her tale, "where you thought they'd not soon be discovered."

"Not for many weeks," she said. "When battles was done an' Father Enguerrand returned."

It should have occurred to me, when I found Sir Simon's clothes, that a woman had placed them in the Easter Sepulcher. A man would have cast them into the enclosure and left them as they fell. A woman would not likely do so, but would fold the garments tidily.

I returned the sack to the lass and looked through the porch entrance, past Arthur, to see if any other soul was about Couzeix. None was. I sent Heloise on her way, believing that I had learned all from her that I was likely to discover. If I thought of other questions for her, I knew where she could be found – behind the decrepit tithe barn pilfering more peas and grain to keep herself and her family alive.

"Sir Simon knew who it was who did for him," Arthur said as we watched Heloise scurry from the village.

"Aye. But we do not. Nor do we know why some man he knew would put a blade through his ribs."

"Wonder if he knew," Arthur mused. "Felt the prick of the dagger an' knew why 'twas used against 'im."

"Mayhap. A man who dies at the hand of another will likely know what he has done, or what he has, which has brought death to him. What we have learned this day may lead us to Sir Simon's murderer. If not, at least the lass will be able to tell Lord Gilbert and Prince Edward that I am innocent of Sir Simon's blood."

"If we can find 'er again when we might need her."

"She'll return to the tithe barn when she is hungry enough."

Arthur and I returned to camp in time for a dinner of pease pottage. What else? Most of the English army made a meal of the same stuff but for the dukes and earls and barons amongst us. I prayed for the speedy success of the Cornish miners.

Lord Gilbert does not like to be kept in the dark about matters in my bailiwick, so after the meal I sought him. I found him entertaining the Earl of Pembroke. They had not dined that day upon pottage.

"Then 'tis sure that Sir Simon was murdered," Lord Gilbert said, when I told him of what I had learned that morning in Couzeix. "Unless the lass spoke false. What of the lass? Is she fair?"

"Some would say so," I replied.

"Not the first time a pert maid caused a man's downfall. But why? Had Sir Simon a rival for the lass's attention?"

"He said, 'You – why are you come here?' moments before he was slain, so 'tis sure he knew his assailant, but possible he did not know why the man was there in the barn."

"There are multiple possibilities," the earl said, "whenever soldiers and a lass are entangled."

"Aye," Lord Gilbert laughed. "Master Hugh will sort them out."

I did not have the same confidence as my employer. Sir Simon knew his slayer, but what of that? He knew many men of the camp. Perhaps a hundred or more. Was I to consider all of these suspect?

Heloise said 'twas nearly dark when Sir Simon was slain, but Sir John said he was told that Sir Simon was seen after nightfall that same evening in company with two others. Someone was not speaking truth. What reason would the lass have to deceive? Why would Sir John's witness lie? I resolved to seek the man and ask him.

I gathered Arthur, Uctred, and Alfred, and set out for Sir John's tents. I found him sitting upon a log, staring glumly into the remaining coals of a dying fire. I remembered then that Sir

Simon was to have been buried that morning. I might also be morose had I just left a child in a churchyard.

I provided Sir John only a brief summary of what I had learned in Couzeix that morning. If Sir Simon knew his assailant, it seemed likely that Sir John would know the man also. Perhaps the fellow was close to both father and son, and would hear gossip of my search for him. I was not close to finding a murderer, but I preferred that the felon not know that.

"Hah," Sir John said when I concluded the summary. "Not surprised a lass is entangled in this business."

If he had thought so at the first, would he have charged me with Sir Simon's death? I reminded Sir John of this.

"Bah... did you fancy the lass also? 'Twas a lass between you and my son, was it not? And you wed her. What was her name?"

"Kate," I said.

"Ah, father a shopkeeper," he said with distaste.

"The man who saw Sir Simon with two others you assumed to be me and my man... I must speak to him."

"Of what? To bring Lord Gilbert's influence upon him to change his witness?"

"If his testimony is true, then the lass speaks false. If the lass speaks true, the man who claimed to see Sir Simon in the night speaks false."

"I see what you are about," Sir John said. "To absolve yourself of murder you will find some innocent friend of my son and charge him."

While inspecting Sir Simon's corpse at the chapel I had thought that Sir John's belief in my guilt was fading. But now it seemed revived, and even the new evidence I had presented to him that day made no difference. Sir John would prefer to believe me the felon who slew his son, and what he preferred, that he would believe. Truth would be inexpedient.

Sir John would not willingly introduce me to the man who claimed to see Sir Simon and two others together in the night. But perhaps he might do so unwillingly. I decided to seek audience with Prince Edward.

I found the prince upon a hill overlooking the river and the walls of Limoges. He was deep in conversation with his brother, John of Gaunt, and occasionally Prince John would point in the direction of the stout wooden shelter which protected the Cornish miners. The roof of the structure was charred black, where the French had dumped burning coals upon it to see if they could ruin it with fire. They had failed, for the heavy planks were green and would not burn. Near to the river was a pile of rocks and dirt which had been excavated from under the wall, and closer to the shelter, yet beyond the range of French crossbowmen, was a pile of beams used to support the excavation till all was ready and the lumber would be set ablaze. This heap of timbers was much smaller than when I last viewed the place. Evidently the miners' work was nearly done.

A third man joined the princes as I watched, and entered the discussion. I learned later that this was that great warrior the Captal de Buch. I had no intention of imposing myself into a debate over military strategy. And debate it seemed to be, for as the three lords spoke, their gestures became animated and Prince John's foot came down upon the earth to assist him in making a point. I and others nearby kept our distance.

Eventually the Captal and Prince John fell silent. Prince Edward looked to each man, said something quietly, and with these words of his the discussion seemed ended. What these warriors disagreed about I never learned. Great lords do not share their differences with bailiffs.

Prince Edward turned and spoke to a valet behind him, and the fellow immediately produced a chair. The prince sat heavily, as if his recent conversation had been debilitating. 'Twas then he glanced up and saw me standing upon the fringe of those who attended him.

The prince motioned me to draw near, and all eyes turned to see who it was Prince Edward had called to his presence.

I bowed and the prince said, "Master Hugh, your herbs have served me well."

"I am pleased, m'lord."

"I am weak, but since Dr. Blackwater made the paste you

advised and mixed it with wine, I have relief. Folk no longer despair of having to be in the same chamber with me, and the bloody flux is less vexatious than before."

"This is good to hear," I said. "There is another matter I would discuss with you, have you the time."

"A matter involving your service to Lord Gilbert as surgeon, or as bailiff?"

"Bailiff, m'lord."

"Thought so. I've no advice for a surgeon. What is it you need of me?"

"Sir John Trillowe is uncooperative in a matter involving his son's death."

"Oh? How so?"

"I have questions for a man who claims to have seen Sir Simon on the night he was slain, but Sir John will not permit me to learn who the fellow is."

"Ah, that would be the man who said 'twas you and one of Lord Gilbert's grooms he saw with Sir Simon?"

"Aye, the same."

"Hmm. Wonder why he doesn't wish for you to speak to the fellow. Perhaps he doesn't exist."

"I admit to the same thoughts," I said.

"So you want me to demand of Sir John that he produce the man?"

"If I cannot question the man, I fear I can go no farther in the investigation of Sir Simon's murder."

"And then it may be your neck stretched. What do you hope to learn?"

"There are discrepancies between the accusation Sir John has made against me and events of which I have learned in the past day."

"Discrepancies? Someone's lying, eh?"

"Perhaps."

"Have you supped?"

I am uncertain what Prince Edward thought I might consume for my supper. Did he know that his army subsisted

112

upon pottage? When I did not immediately respond he said, "Nay, of course not. Come, you will take bread and meat with me and I will hear more of this matter... what you have learned this day."

Roasted boar and wheaten loaves for dinner. More roasted boar and wheaten loaves for supper. The same the next day and the day after, with an occasional fish from the river on fast days to break the monotony. The great lords before Limoges ate as tedious a diet as we their underlings, although we would gladly have changed places with the barons, whereas they would surely not.

I thought of Arthur and Uctred and Alfred and William consuming cold pottage for their supper whilst I ate roasted pork and wheaten loaves and licked greasy fingers, and nearly felt guilty for my good fortune. Nearly. What would my father say if he had known that his youngest son had dined with royalty? What will my Kate say when I tell her of this meal? The poor Oxford student studying at Balliol College has come far.

Prince Edward plied me with questions about Couzeix, the well and the church, and Heloise. He could consume roasted pork and wheaten loaves whenever he wished, so a slab of roasted flesh cooled upon his trencher as he asked me one question after another. I, on the other hand, was more interested in the meal than relieving the prince's curiosity, so found myself required to speak with my mouth full of pork or go hungry. I was taught better than to speak at table with a mouth full of food. I hope Prince Edward does not think me ill bred.

The prince's curiosity and my hunger were sated at nearly the same time. Edward promised to send a valet to Sir John forthwith to require cooperation of him in the matter of Sir Simon's death. I returned to Lord Gilbert's tents, there to wait, digest my supper, and allow Sir John time to reflect upon Prince Edward's demand.

'Twas but an hour till dark when I roused myself to seek Sir John. The prince had required him to aid my investigation, but I prefer caution to foolish valor. Especially after having been wounded several times in Lord Gilbert's service. I took Arthur, Alfred, and Uctred with me.

Sir John was not pleased to see me. Nothing new or unusual about that. He sat upon a bench before his tent, scowled at my approach, and refused to stand or to greet me. I decided to be blunt.

"You have received Prince Edward's command?" I said.

"Aye," he growled.

Six men of his band stood about. He called to one, and the fellow approached.

"Here is the man you seek," Sir John said. "Ask what you will. He will tell you what he has already told me."

A youth of perhaps eighteen years stepped before me and tugged a forelock which dangled below the cap which he wore tilted over one ear in Sir Simon's fashion.

"What is your name?" I asked.

"Alan."

"Come with me. Prince Edward has assigned me the task of discovering a felon, and Sir John believes that you may have seen the man. Or men."

I led Alan to Lord Gilbert's tents and bade him sit upon a bench. "You saw Sir Simon in the evening before he was slain, in company with two others. So Sir John has said. Is this so?"

"Aye. You an' that great fellow," he said, pointing toward Arthur.

"What of the clock was this?"

"Uh… third hour of the night."

"There was no moon yet risen, and 'twas clouded. How could you see who accompanied Sir Simon, or even know 'twas Sir Simon that you saw?"

"Wore 'is yellow cap, didn't 'e?" Alan said. "Easy enough to see, even in the dark."

"Other men wear yellow caps. Show me where it was you saw these three men."

Alan stood, glanced about as if seeking his bearings, then said, "'Twas this way," and led me toward the river. Couzeix lay in the opposite direction.

Nearly two hundred paces beyond my tent the youth

stopped, cast about as if seeking some landmark, then said, "Here."

We were near to the ridge from which could be seen, in the day, the walls of Limoges and the work to undermine the fortress.

"Why would Sir Simon, or any man, come here in the dark?" I asked. "There is little enough to draw a man to this place in the day."

"Dunno," Alan shrugged.

"Why were you here to see him? Did you follow him?"

"Why would I do so?"

"I cannot imagine, which is why I asked. You saw Sir Simon and two others here, you say. Where did they then go?"

"Dunno. Dark, wasn't it?"

"Light enough that you could identify Sir Simon and Arthur and me, yet so dark that you could not see where three men went from this place?"

In past investigations I have found it helpful to invoke Lord Gilbert's name when I think a man might attempt to deceive me. This is often effective in persuading folk to speak the truth when they would rather not. Prince Edward has greater authority than Lord Gilbert. Mention of his name could do no harm, I decided.

"Prince Edward has charged me with discovering the truth of this matter. He will not be pleased if I tell him that you have been unhelpful."

"But I speak true," Alan protested.

"Nay, you do not. Do you know where Sir Simon's corpse was found?"

"Some village nearby, where you cast 'im into the well."

"The place is called Couzeix. It lies nearly a mile that way." I pointed past the English army's tents, now nearly invisible in the dusk. "Why would Sir Simon have come here, when he was found in the opposite direction?"

"You took 'im there."

"What? I did murder here, then Arthur and I carried Sir Simon around the camp, unseen by any other? Or do you claim that he walked willingly with me from here to Couzeix? Why would he do so? He hated me."

"And you hated him, so you slew him."

"Nay. I did not hate Sir Simon. I disliked him, as did many others, I have learned, but I did not hate him. There is a difference. Had I slain him here I could have carried him to yon river and dropped him in. 'Tis but a few hundred paces beyond that hill. Why bear him a mile in the other direction? And if he hated me so, why would he accompany me and Arthur to Couzeix, or here for that matter, in the dark of night? Much that you have said makes no sense. Tomorrow I will inform Prince Edward of your deceit. He has men skilled at drawing truth from those who would hide it."

I did not need to say how such men extract truth from those who try to withhold it. The lad became white.

"What, if anything, did you see here? You did not see me. Did you see Sir Simon – here, or anywhere?"

Alan was silent, perhaps considering the rack and similar devices.

"Sir John said I was to tell you I was witness to you an' Sir Simon together."

"When did he demand this of you? Yesterday?"

"Nay. Just before you came to camp, not an hour past."

"Sir John claimed that I was seen in company with Sir Simon two days past. Why has he demanded of you that you say so just now?"

The youth was again silent for some time, then finally said, "Old Ranulf would not be believed."

"Some man named Ranulf is he who claimed to see me with Sir Simon? Why would you be believed and he not?"

"Old, is Ranulf, an' don't see well."

"So if he said that he saw me with Sir Simon he'd not be believed, but you would?"

"Aye."

"Return to Sir John. Tell him I will speak to Ranulf tomorrow at the third hour."

"Sir John will be displeased."

"With you? Aye, he will. Would you rather that Prince Edward be displeased with you?"

Alan said no more, but stumbled away upon the darkening path.

"Wonder why Sir John is so determined to prove us guilty of Sir Simon's death," Arthur said. "You suppose he knows who the felon is, an' don't want the man known?"

"Perhaps, but I doubt it so. I bested Sir Simon, and a father does not like to see a son foiled. If the man who slew Sir Simon cannot be discovered, Sir John will accept punishment of the man who prevailed twice over his son."

Chapter 11

Next morn I broke my fast with cold pottage and watered ale, then with Arthur, Uctred, and Alfred again accompanying me, set out for Sir John's tents. Perhaps the cause was the tasteless pottage and stale ale, but I was in a foul mood.

Sir John's hair and beard were unkempt. 'Twas not yet the third hour and he had just risen from his pallet. So his mood was as baleful as mine, and he tilted his head strangely to one side, as if a great weight was hung from his ear.

"Where is Ranulf?" I said.

Sir John cleared his throat and spat upon the ground near to my feet. Here was a message delivered and received.

"Ranulf is old, and does not rise early from his bed," Sir John growled.

"Alan saw no man with Sir Simon. 'Twas Ranulf who did so, he said."

This was apparently a revelation to Sir John. I suspect that Alan went straight to his bed the night before rather than present his lord with the infelicitous news that I did not believe him and had learned of Ranulf from him.

Three grooms sat about a smoldering fire. They had looked up when we appeared and were watching my brief conversation with Sir John intently. Sir John turned to one of these and said, "Fetch Ranulf." The man stood from his log and hurried away.

Ranulf did not immediately appear. When he did so he was as disheveled as Sir John and rubbing sleep from his eyes. The man had grown old and toothless in Sir John's service. Likely he was once young and full of vigor, but now he was bent and scrawny. His hair was a tangled grey circlet about his bare skull, and his eyes were pale with cataracts. I wondered why such a doddering fellow was a part of Sir John's company on campaign. And this was the man who saw me and Arthur with Sir Simon in the night? I doubted that he could identify a man in daylight from more than ten paces away. Indeed, he seemed to look past me when I spoke to him, able to see clearly only those things and men not directly before his gaze. 'Tis no wonder Sir John did not wish to name the fellow as he who saw me with Sir Simon.

I required of Ranulf that he follow me to Lord Gilbert's tents. I wanted him away from Sir John's influence, and in a place where his master could not hear the replies he made to my questions. He looked inquiringly to Sir John, as if to ask if he must do this, and Sir John replied by turning and entering his tent.

I sat the fellow upon a bench before my tent, walked a few paces from him, and held three fingers before my chest. I asked Ranulf how many fingers he saw. The man turned his gaze aside and squinted in the direction of my voice.

"How many fingers am I holding before you?" I repeated.

After more squinting and shifting himself upon the bench the man replied. "Four," he said.

"Three," I replied. "You cannot count fingers whilst it is day, but you claim to have seen me with Sir Simon after darkness had fallen, on a cloudy night with no moon till past midnight. How can this be so?"

"Heard you an' Sir Simon."

"You recognize voices?"

"Aye. Don't see so well, but me ears is good. Knew Sir Simon's voice."

"You have not heard me speak until this hour. Why did you tell Sir John 'twas me who accompanied Sir Simon?"

"'Cause of what you said, an' what Sir Simon replied."

"What was said to Sir Simon?"

"'Best keep your dagger sheathed next time,' you said. An' Sir Simon said, 'Next time you'll not have it from me.' All Sir John's men know of you seizin' Sir Simon's dagger. That's 'ow I knew 'twas you with 'im."

"And you claim that, although you cannot see well, you heard the conversation clearly?"

"Aye, I did."

"At what hour did you hear this?"

119

"Why d'you ask? You was there, speakin' to Sir Simon."

"Nay. 'Twas not me nor any other of Lord Gilbert's men that you heard. And why were you following Sir Simon about in the night?"

"Wasn't. Goin' to yon wood to relieve myself an' come upon you an' Sir Simon goin' same way."

"How many paces were you from Sir Simon when you heard this conversation?"

"Dunno. Don't see so well."

"Hazard a guess."

Ranulf was silent for a moment. Perhaps he understood what I was about to do. "Ten paces," he finally said.

"Arthur," I said, "walk ten paces toward that wood, then say something. Face away from us, as Sir Simon would have been turned away from Ranulf if he was behind and following Sir Simon."

Arthur did so. "This fellow is likely deaf as well as blind," he said. I could only just make out the words myself.

"What did my man say?" I asked Ranulf.

"He said I'm near dead an' a blunderer."

I turned to Arthur, who had rejoined us. "Repeat what you said."

He did so.

"He never said that," Ranulf protested.

"Aye, I did so, an' true it is. You hear little an' see less."

"'Tis my belief," I said, "that you heard nothing of daggers, either sheathed or otherwise. After you heard Sir Simon speak to his companion, which way then did they go? Could you see that?"

"Toward the sun, which was near to setting. I could see that well enough."

Sir John had told all that I was seen with Sir Simon after sunset. Why? Had Ranulf changed his story? Had he been told to do so? Did it make a difference?

Ranulf pointed as he spoke, in the direction of Couzeix.

"And two men were with Sir Simon, so you say. Did they both speak?"

"Dunno. That great lout is ever with you, so Sir John does say."

"So shadows were long, 'twas evening, you could see little, and you heard two voices. But you did not see three men. Is this not so?"

"Aye," he admitted.

"Did you hear any other conversation?"

I asked this, but did not expect a helpful answer. I was wrong. Again.

"Aye. Sir Simon an' you, or whoever 'twas, began to speak in low voices, like they knew some man might be about. Mayhap they seen me. But then the other fellow cried out, 'Go your own way, then. I'm done with you.'"

"This was a shout? And not Sir Simon?"

"Aye. Couldn't mistake that. Whole camp might've 'eard, was that loud."

Ranulf's ears functioned little better than his eyes, but I was inclined to believe his report. Even an aged man might hear plainly words bellowed in anger.

If Sir Simon then went his own way, where was that? Couzeix? And where did the other man go? Was it he who surprised Sir Simon and the lass? If so, 'twas likely he who slew Sir Simon. What did the two men say in hushed tones which caused them to part in anger? If I knew that, I might know the felon who came upon Sir Simon and Heloise.

Whoever the man was, he and Sir Simon had been friends, else they would not have gone off together in the evening. Friends may fall out, and it seemed now likely that this had happened the evening Sir Simon was slain.

I admonished Ranulf that if he remembered anything else of that encounter with Sir Simon and the other, he must seek me and tell me of it. Arthur and I then led him back to Sir John's camp. I suppose he would have found his way on his own. As we returned I asked why Sir John required an aged man with clouded vision to accompany him on this campaign.

"Didn't demand it of me. I wished to go."

"Why so? You are of an age when a man might rest and savor the few days he has remaining before he meets the Lord Christ."

"When you have become old you will understand," Ranulf said. "I was with Sir John at Poitiers. No man wishes to find himself useless. I'll die soon, I know this. May as well be in battle as in bed."

Perhaps when I am old and decrepit I will understand better Ranulf's view.

Sir John stood when we approached. "So... have you threatened my man so to make him change his report?"

"No threat, but his tale is now somewhat unlike what it was. Ranulf can neither see nor hear well, but you have charged me with felony upon his witness. He could not see who was with Sir Simon Saturday eve, nor could he hear what was said. You put words into his mouth to entangle me in your son's murder, even before you knew if his death was mischance or murder. Do you hate me so that you would see me hang rather than the true malefactor? Or did you think that you could be rid of me, then seek the true villain when I was in my grave?"

As I spoke I saw that Sir John yet held his head askew. He was pale, his brow furrowed with puzzlement or pain.

"Thought it was likely you or some other of Lord Gilbert's men who slew him. You had cause, I know."

"So I did. Others did also. Few men esteemed your son, I have learned."

Sir John shrugged, admitting silently to the truth of the assertion, then reached a hand to his right ear and cupped it gently. I saw him grimace.

"You are in pain?"

"Aye."

"Your ear aches?"

"It does."

"For how long have you been vexed?"

"Two days."

"And the pain grows greater?"

"Aye. Can't sleep for the hurt."

That explained Sir John's disheveled appearance when I approached his tents earlier. Indeed, his countenance was little improved even now that the day was no longer new.

"You bein' a surgeon, have you a remedy for such an affliction?"

The thought crossed my mind that Sir John, who had plotted evil against me, should suffer for his iniquity. But I then remembered a scripture I had read in my Bible shortly before departing Bampton. The Lord Christ commanded that we not return evil for evil, but do good to those who would use us ill. This, I admit, I did not want to do. I suspect that the Lord Christ did not wish to die for my sins, either, but He did so.

"There are potions which may sometimes ease such discomfort," I said.

"Sometimes?" Sir John replied.

"Not all aches are caused by the same disorder."

"Have you the potions of which you speak?"

"I have with me some of the ingredients. I came with Lord Gilbert prepared to deal with wounds and injuries, not earaches and scrofulous sores and such."

"I will be much obliged to you if you can offer me relief," Sir John said softly. He understood how little he warranted my service after the accusation he had made against me, but pain drove him to abase himself and beg my charity. The ache must have been severe for him to do so.

"I have within my tent a chest which contains herbs that may bring you relief. I will go and prepare an ointment. You know where Lord Gilbert's camp is."

Sir John nodded, then grimaced as his ache reminded him to hold his head quiet.

"Come to my tent in an hour. I will have the balm ready."

I had within my chest three of the ingredients I would need to treat Sir John's affliction: root of monkshood, savin leaves, and seeds of henbane. I crushed a dozen henbane seeds in a small cup, then ground savin leaves and a small fragment of monkshood

123

root into the mixture till all was as fine as grains of pepper. This I then blended with a syrup of crushed poppy seeds which I make each year from the poppies that grow in wild profusion in fields about Bampton.

I was concluding the preparation when I heard Arthur greet Sir John. Sir John's pain had driven him to my tent early. I had warned Arthur that the knight would soon arrive and not to take his coming amiss.

Arthur held the tent flap aside for Sir John to enter. I told the knight to recline upon my pallet with his aching ear up, then took a small funnel and poured some of my concoction into his ear. To keep the liquid from draining from Sir John's ear, I folded a small scrap of wool and stuffed it into the ear. I told Sir John he could then rise.

"That's all?" he said.

"I have prepared an ointment which is often effective for afflictions like yours. Here is a small vial of what remains. Have a groom pour some into your ear morning and night, then replace the scrap of wool so the potion will remain to do its work."

Sir John took the vial and said, "What is owed for this relief?"

Sir John is a wealthy man, and deserves no consideration from me, so I was tempted to ask an excessive fee. But I thought better of it. What good a heavy purse if it drags a man down to hell?

"Three pence," I said.

Sir John produced the coins and turned to leave with his vial, but I asked him to again be seated. He did so with a quizzical expression upon his face.

I said, "You have heard, I suppose, what Ranulf thought he heard of the conversation between your son and some other man. Much of this was mistaken, as you well know, for Ranulf can neither see nor hear well. But I give credence to one thing he claims to have heard. He said that Sir Simon seemed to part from the other man in ill temper. The other fellow shouted, 'Go your own way, then. I'm done with you.'

"If some man in anger said that he was done with Sir Simon, that man must have had to do with him until that falling out. And when Sir Simon left your camp Saturday evening it is likely he would have done so in company with a friend.

"Who were your son's closest companions? Do any of these now seem out of sorts, or look away rather than meet your eye?"

Sir John sat upon my pallet absent-mindedly stroking his aching ear as he considered my question. He did not soon reply. I believe he found it distasteful to provide me with the names of Sir Simon's friends, and thereby cast suspicion upon them, when likely all but one were innocent of his son's blood. Perhaps all were, but I doubted so.

"John de Boys and Simon were friends. Roger Wrawe and Richard Heryng also." Sir John then fell silent. Three friends. I was not surprised that Sir John could name no more. And if Sir Simon's friends resembled him, dealing with them would be vexatious. Perhaps it was well that the man had few friends. 'Twould make my work the easier.

"Are any of these knights?" I asked.

"Nay. Gentlemen. John, I think, will be knighted soon. Roger and Richard are but lads."

"Say nothing to these men of this conversation, but watch their behavior."

Sir John slowly shook his head. His beard, already grey when he was sheriff of Oxford some years past, had grown long and unkempt whilst on this campaign, and was now nearly white.

"Can't believe one of them would have pitched him into a well," he said.

"Easier to believe it of me, eh?"

"When a man dies, 'tis always assumed he was slain at the hands of an enemy, not a friend."

"True enough," I said. "But friends fall out, and I believe this has happened. The man who murdered Sir Simon was one of the three you have named, I'll wager, or some other whose name has not yet occurred to you. If some other man comes to mind, send me word."

"What do you intend?"

"I do not yet know."

This was true. But had I already a scheme in mind, I would not have told Sir John of it.

An hour later I had consumed my dinner – pottage, of course – and was considering methods whereby I might ferret out truth from Sir Simon's friends, when I heard a muffled roar from over the ridge beyond which lay Limoges.

Arthur and I exchanged glances, then rose and hurried to learn what had caused the clamor. As we topped the hill I saw wisps of smoke from near the wall and understood what this meant. The Cornish miners had completed their excavation and the shaft's support beams had been set alight. The timbers were recently hewn from a nearby wood, and so were green. What began as grey wisps issuing from the shed became a thickening cloud as the blaze began to gnaw at the damp beams.

Lord Gilbert had said that undermining the wall, then setting the supports afire, was not assured of success in bringing down the wall. And even if the work achieved this goal, the fire might burn for several days before it consumed the beams and collapsed the wall.

Nearly all of the English army was by this time upon the hill overlooking Limoges. A few knights and men-at-arms had donned their armor, archers leaned upon their bows, and many infantrymen wore their padded aketons and grasped poleaxes and halberds. All was ready if and when the wall collapsed.

I stood watching alongside the others, but I was still turning my puzzle over in my mind. Heloise had placed Sir Simon's chauces and braes in the Easter Sepulcher, but when I found the garments no shoes or dagger were there. Had the lass taken these? If so, why not take the other clothing also? Or did the murderer take shoes and dagger?

If the felon was a friend to Sir Simon he would not wear the shoes or be seen with the dagger, but mayhap he concealed them in some hidden place, to use or sell at some future time.

I looked about at the English warriors who waited

expectantly to see a section of Limoges's wall crumble. I saw some of Sir John's men, but he seemed not to be among them. Perhaps his aching ear caused him to remain in his tent. If so, he might be the only man of his company to do so. This presented an opportunity if 'twas so.

I gathered Arthur and Uctred and told them we must hasten back to the camp. Their eyes questioned this. Surely they wished to remain. Who would want to miss seeing a city wall tumble? How many times in a lifetime might a man view such a spectacle?

I trotted down the ridge with Arthur and Uctred puffing behind. Running is not an exercise in which Arthur excels. Uctred may once have been swift upon his feet, but the years have taken a toll. I slowed to a rapid walk before we arrived at the tents so as not to outpace my companions.

Arthur and Uctred were yet breathless when we stopped before Sir John's tent. While they caught their breath I called to Sir John, unsure if he was within or not, and unwilling to enter without his consent.

I called his name a second time and heard the rustle of fabric and a stifled groan. Sir John, or some page perhaps, was within, but I thought it unlikely that a page would have cause to moan in pain.

"Who is it?" Sir John said. "Who's there?"

"Master Hugh. I must have words with you. 'Tis urgent."

Sir John was silent for some time. I wondered if he had swooned. "Very well. Enter," he finally said.

I told Arthur and Uctred to remain at the entrance to the tent and call out if any man approached, then drew the flap aside and entered. Sir John sat upon his bed, his features yet contorted with pain.

"The potion has not succeeded," he said, assuming that to be the reason for my appearance.

"'Twill need several days to do its work," I replied. "I should have warned you of that. 'Tis why I sent the vial with you and told you to apply the ointment twice each day.

"But I am come upon another matter. You alone of your

company are at camp rather than watching to learn if the wall of Limoges will fall."

"Aye. I am useless in a fight as I now am."

"In which of your tents do de Boys, Wrawe, and Heryng sleep?"

"What do you intend?"

"I told you of Sir Simon's clothes being found in the Easter Sepulcher of the Couzeix church. But neither his shoes nor his dagger have been found. Perhaps the man who slew him took them. I cannot identify his shoes, but I know his dagger. It might be profitable to search his friends' possessions. If Sir Simon's dagger is found where it ought not be, we will know who sent him to meet the Lord Christ."

Sir John did not reply for some time. Perhaps he thought such a search unjust, or mayhap his aching ear drove other thoughts from his mind. But after a few minutes of silence he stood, somewhat unsteadily, and walked to the entrance of his tent. He stood in the opening and pointed to two tents twenty or so paces from his own. "John and another sleep in the tent with the blue banner," he said. "Richard and Roger in the tent with the green flap at the entrance."

Sir John said no more, but stumbled to his bed and immediately reclined upon it, his head resting upon the pillow so that the afflicted ear pointed toward the heavens. This was surely the least distressing position for his ear, but also aided in keeping the syrup where it would best serve to reduce his pain.

Would a man keep a stolen dagger in his chest? Where else would he keep it? Perhaps bury it in the earth under his tent? If 'twas in the bottom of a chest the dagger might also avoid detection if the chest was locked. And most such chests are. Mine is.

Sir John could demand that his retainers open their chests to me for examination. But if I found no dagger in the chests belonging to de Boys, Wrawe, and Heryng, any other man who had done murder would be warned that I was searching and would remove Sir Simon's dagger from his chest, if that was where it was, and any further search of such chests would be fruitless.

Chests are similar and so are locks. I drew the key to my chest from my pouch, bid Arthur and Uctred follow, and hurried to the tent which John de Boys shared with some other. At the entrance I bid Uctred keep watch whilst Arthur and I entered.

I told Arthur what we sought, and told him to examine the ground beneath us as I tried the chests. Nearly all of the English tents had been raised upon a grassy meadow. The vegetation was long since beaten down both inside and outside the tents, but enough sod remained that if any man had buried a dagger or shoes within his tent, the disturbed earth might indicate the place.

I tried my key in the lock of one of the chests, not knowing which of the two belonged to John de Boys. After some poking and twisting I felt the key turn.

The chest held clothing and a small sack of coins. I excavated its contents to the very bottom and found no shoes or dagger. But was this de Boys' chest?

Arthur concluded his examination of sod under the tent and watched as I unsuccessfully tried to turn the key in the second chest. I finally gave up the exercise and told Arthur that we would seek the chests in the other tent Sir John had identified.

Once again Arthur went to examining the soil whilst I tried the locks. Both chests eventually yielded to me, but I found no dagger in either. One chest contained a pair of well-worn shoes. I doubted that Sir Simon would have possessed or worn shoes so shabby.

Not all good ideas succeed, which may not mean that they were bad ideas. Unless the chest I was unable to open belonged to John de Boys and contained a dagger, the notion that I might discover a felon by probing the depths of three chests seemed a failure. I was not, however, ready to abandon the scheme. Perhaps there might be a way that I could discover the contents of the unopened chest. But what that might be I had no idea.

Chapter 12

Arthur, Uctred, and I departed Sir John's tents and set out for the ridge overlooking the river and Limoges. We found the scene there much as we had left it an hour earlier, except that perhaps the smoke billowing from the shaft under the wall was thicker. Did this mean that the timbers of the shaft were burning more fiercely?

I stood with three thousand others and watched the breeze wreathe Limoges's wall with smoke. The French soldiers who had peered at their besiegers were absent from the section of wall above the burning shaft. Smoke no doubt burned their eyes. Or perhaps they did not wish to be atop a wall which might collapse at any moment.

Most of my companions would have thoughts of battle and glory and victory, and the gentlemen and knights amongst them surely had thoughts of ransom as well.

Not so with me. I could not rid my mind of the chest which I could not open. I considered and discarded several notions whereby a locked chest might be breached. All of these involved acts which would mar the chest. If I found Sir Simon's dagger in it, the damage done in opening the chest would not matter, but if no dagger was there the chest's owner would be outraged, and rightly so. And word would soon pass through Sir John's tents that I was searching through men's chests. If Sir Simon's dagger was hid in any other chest it would immediately find another home.

Keys. They are some different from each other, yet similar, and do the same work. My key opened three of four locks. Was it possible that another key, slightly different from my own, might be enough unlike mine that it would open the fourth chest? Sir John would surely have a locked chest, and a key.

I decided that an experiment with Sir John's key would not require Arthur and Uctred to be present, so told them that they could remain, watching for a tumbling wall, whilst I returned to the camp.

I hurried from the hill to Sir John's tent and found him yet abed. But this time, when I entered his tent, he was not quite so obviously discomfited. Mayhap the syrup was doing its work.

"That chest," I said, pointing to his large, iron-bound oaken box. "Have you a lock and key for it?"

The chest sat at the end of his bed and was turned so that I could not see if it was fitted with a lock.

"Of course. What man of property would take a chest upon campaign which he could not secure?"

"I need the key for a few minutes."

"What?" he replied with indignation. "You intend to pry into my possessions? You believe my son's dagger to be within my chest, and that I had to do with his death?"

"Nay. I wish to learn whether or not your key will open another chest."

"Whose?"

"Within the tent with the blue banner are two chests. One I was able to open using the key to my own chest. Sir Simon's dagger was not within. The other chest I could not open. Which of the chests belongs to John de Boys I know not, but would like to know if Sir Simon's dagger might be hid in the chest I could not open."

Sir John reached for a pouch which dangled from a tent pole and produced from it a key. He handed it to me wordlessly. I noticed that he did not seem so unsteady as but two hours past.

I walked quickly to John de Boys' tent, glanced about to see if any man saw me, then entered it.

I had no more success with Sir John's key than I had with my own. The lock and chest were of quality, well made of the best oak and iron, using the newest methods of construction.

"No success," I said to Sir John as I returned his key.

"I could demand of the owner that he open his chest to me," Sir John said.

"Would he do so? 'Twould be easy enough for him to claim

that he had misplaced his key. A day later he will have found the key, but no dagger would be found in the chest, even if it may be there now."

"Oh... aye. Well, if he will not open the chest I could order it smashed open."

"'Tis well made, and expensive. If no dagger is found within, you would need to pay the man for his destroyed chest. He would likely require four or five shillings."

Sir John thought about this expense, then said, "Is there no other way? Perhaps a man could steal into the tent in the night, whilst they slept, and fetch the key."

"If he knew where it was kept," I replied. "'Twould not be easy to find in the dark, even if one knew where to seek it. And in the day the fellow will have the key upon his person."

"Oh... aye," Sir John muttered, and sat upon his bed. "You do believe my son slain by a friend?"

"What is known points to such a conclusion, but which friend I cannot tell, nor can I think of a way to learn so, if I cannot discover his dagger in some other man's possession."

A few minutes later, walking back to the ridge overlooking Limoges, a way to open the reluctant chest occurred to me. The hinges of most chests are held in place with rivets. I had heard of screws, and how they work to join objects together, but had never seen such a device in use. Until today. As I walked the path and considered the frustrating chest, it came to me that the hinges were fixed to box and lid with screws. Rivets cannot be drawn from their position without destroying them, but from what I had heard of screws, they are infinitely reusable, and if withdrawn and replaced leave no sign that they have been tampered with.

I turned in the path and hastened back to the blue-bannered tent.

How does one withdraw a screw? This I asked myself as I bent over the chest. I saw that slots crossed the head of each screw, and that the heads were much like rivets or nails but for the slot. 'Twas the slots which had told that the fasteners were screws and not rivets or nails.

I unsheathed my dagger and fitted the blade near the point into a slot in one of the screws. The screw resisted for a moment, then broke free. A few more turns with the dagger and I was able to complete drawing it from the chest with my fingers.

Each hinge was held in place with three screws through the lid and three into the chest. I removed the six screws which fastened hinges to lid, carefully set the lid aside, and searched the depths of the chest. I found Sir Simon's dagger wrapped in a linen kirtle and hid under cotehardies, chauces, tunics, and other apparel, and a fat purse full of silver coins. John de Boys came from a wealthy family.

The discovery so occupied me that I did not hear the man approach his tent. And my back was to the opening as I knelt over the chest. The first I knew that another was within the tent was an enraged shout.

"What are you doing with my chest?" John de Boys cried. I recognized him as the man who had brought payment for Sir Simon's dagger, and who had accompanied Sir Simon on the evening at Leeds Castle when the knight had struck me. This same man had also found Sir Simon's corpse in Couzeix's well.

My dagger lay upon the sod where I had placed it after loosening the last screw. I seized it and leaped to my feet, two daggers in hand. In my right hand I held Sir Simon's dagger, in my left my own.

De Boys, startled, had not yet drawn his own dagger, or his sword, which hung useless from his belt. He found himself unready, and facing a man with a blade in each hand. He backed slowly toward the tent opening.

"Sir John," de Boys shouted. "The murderer is caught, and is a thief as well."

"The murderer has been caught, true enough," I said. "And we both now know who the felon is. Here is Sir Simon's dagger, found in your chest. I know it well, as does Sir John, I'm sure."

"You placed it there, within my chest, to escape the consequences of your felony and shift blame to me."

"'Go your own way, then. I am done with you.' Ranulf heard

these words spoken to Sir Simon the night that he was slain. Why would I say such a thing, when all men know I had as little to do with Sir Simon as possible?"

De Boys seemed to deflate before my eyes, as a pig's bladder inflated for sport pricked with a pin.

"How is it you have Sir Simon's dagger hid in your chest?" I asked.

"F-found it," he stammered.

"Oh? Where? And why did you not tell Sir John of the discovery?"

"Found it near that village, Couzeix, when we all went seeking for Simon."

"And told no one of your discovery? That does not seem credible. I suspect that Sir John will not believe such a tale."

"Didn't tell Sir John... because I thought to sell the dagger. Worth three shillings, thereabouts."

I lifted his purse from the chest, jingling the coins within, then said, "A man possessing this purse needed another two or three shillings so badly that he would confiscate a murdered man's property? Who would believe such a tale?

"The lass saw you, you know," I said. She could not, she had said, recognize Sir Simon's murderer, for 'twas too dark, but de Boys did not know this.

"Why did you slay him?" I asked. "Did you want the lass for yourself?"

De Boys turned from me and faced the entry to his tent. I thought he was about to flee, but not so.

"He was unfaithful," de Boys said softly. "Over and over again. Said we'd always be together, but then he found that trollop in Couzeix."

"So you followed him there to slay him?"

"Meant to slay the maid he went to meet, but he heard me and spoke so harshly I struck him instead when he rose to face me."

"You allowed the lass to run away?"

"Couldn't credit what I'd done. Just stood there while Simon kicked about in the straw and then lay still. The lass ran away while I was in a daze."

"When did you think of putting him in the well?"

"Knew he'd be found if folk searched the village, and near naked as he was, there'd be questions. His chauces and braes were nearby, but I had not the heart to try to put them on him. Men might have seen us together that evening. Thought if he was in the well he'd not be found. Not soon, anyway. Dragged him to it, then broke a branch from a bush to sweep away the track of his heels in the dust."

"But next morn you found him in the well," I said.

"Couldn't bear the thought of him being there."

"There was a bucket at the well. I found a bloodstain upon it. How so?"

"Dunno. I tripped over something in the dark as I lifted Sir Simon to the lip of the well. Mayhap 'twas a bucket."

"What of Ranulf? Why did he accuse me of Sir Simon's murder?"

"Paid him three pence to tell Sir John 'twas you. Knew you an' Sir Simon were enemies."

De Boys turned from the entrance to his tent and sat upon his pallet. "I knew, when you came nosing about, that 'twas likely you would find me out."

The man seemed almost relieved that this was so. He had incriminated himself with little prodding from me, as if he found solace in no longer bearing the burden of his sins alone.

"I am a dead man," he said, "and my family is ruined. When men learn of why I slew Sir Simon they will laugh at my name. They'll make sport of my brothers. My father will be disgraced.

"I will hang, I know. 'Tis my father's shame which troubles me. I deserve what will come. He does not, nor my mother. My guilt is not theirs."

This was so, but reputation is not always based upon wise judgment – it is rather a product of men's prejudice. What men might think of John de Boys should not color their opinion of his family, but likely would.

"There will be a battle soon," I said. "Why did you return to your tent?"

"For my basinet," he replied. "Others are also making ready. The wall will soon collapse."

This was likely so. From outside the tent I heard voices where but a short time ago there was only silence. Men were making final preparations for battle, gathering weapons and armor.

"Will you tell Sir John of my guilt soon?"

"Aye... I will see justice done. Your sins have found you out. But mayhap there is a way to do justice for Sir Simon which will not abase your father. I care little for your reputation. Your perversion is repugnant to me. But your father should not bear the consequence of your sin."

De Boys had been sitting upon his bed, staring at his feet. My words caused him to look up.

"You intended to retrieve your basinet and return, ready to fight if the wall tumbled?"

De Boys nodded.

"If you plunge through the rubble of the fallen wall, in the van, you will be in a dangerous situation. It may be that you will be slain in the combat. Your father and mother will be grieved at this loss, I'm sure, but others will honor your father as a man whose son died a heroic death."

I said no more, but watched de Boys as his emotions played out across his face. He knew that he would soon die. I had given him a choice as to how death would meet him.

"If I die in battle you will not tell Sir John of my guilt?"

"I will tell him only that he may rest easy; that justice has been done."

"What if he demands to know how this could be so?"

"I serve Lord Gilbert Talbot. Sir John cannot demand a thing from me if Lord Gilbert disallows it."

De Boys said no more, but reached for his basinet, adjusted his tunic where it had become wrinkled against his armor, took a last look at me and his open chest, then bent to depart his tent.

"You cannot escape death," I reminded him. "No man can do so. But you may escape sin. To those who confess their wickedness the Lord Christ is merciful, though men are not. The Lord Christ judges a man, I think, not by where he has been, but by where he is going – the way he faces."

De Boys stopped at the entrance to his tent, as if considering this thought, then strode away. What he thought of my words I could not tell.

I wondered if he would go to the scene of future combat and accept my suggestion, or seek his horse and flee. I looked through the tent entrance and watched as de Boys walked up the muddy path which led to the ridge overlooking Limoges, where he would join the assembled warriors awaiting a fallen wall. I followed.

Night came upon us and the mine under the wall glowed, yet the stones did not fall. Some men drifted away, to seek slumber in their tents. Most remained, unwilling to miss seeing a city wall topple – if, indeed, the wall would accommodate our wishes and do so.

It did, but I was among those who sought Morpheus and returned to my pallet about midnight. Near to dawn I heard a great roar, a thunder of collapsing stone and shouting men, and knew, even in my somnolent condition, what the uproar must mean.

Dr. Blackwater, Prince Edward's physician, had prepared a tent where, when battle commenced, the wounded would be taken. I hurried there with a pouch of instruments and another of physics useful in the treatment of wounds. The physician was at his tent already, awaiting custom, and a moment later we were joined by another surgeon, Thomas Calne, whose name I had heard but whom I had not met. He served Sir Walter Cressy, and seemed well prepared and businesslike.

Blackwater's tent was in view of the combat, so I was able to watch as men clambered over the fallen segment of wall. As yet Blackwater, Calne, and I had no employment, but that would soon change.

There was little for the Welsh archers to do. Most of them held back upon the lower slope and remained alert for any face which appeared atop an undamaged section of wall. Such an appearance was greeted with a dozen or more arrows and the man vanished.

Knights and men-at-arms continued to mount the fallen stones of the wall and pass through the breach. From more than one hundred paces away I could hear the shouts of inflamed men and the clash of metal upon metal as sword met sword.

A moment later I saw the great doors of the east gatehouse swing open and the portcullis rise. Men-at-arms who had scaled the fallen segment of wall had fought their way to the gatehouse and opened the portal to their comrades. What had been a trickle of English soldiers entering Limoges now became a torrent.

Within a few moments a reverse flow began. I saw a man stagger through the gatehouse holding a hand to a bloodied shoulder. His aketon had not saved him from a wound. I hurried to the surgery tent where other casualties would soon join the fellow.

I spent the next five hours reassembling broken men. When the last of the wounds were stitched closed and bathed with wine, Calne and I had nearly consumed our supply of silken thread. Blackwater was of little use. Physicians are oft unwilling to redden their hands with the blood of the injured and wounded, preferring to sniff a man's urine from a distance and prescribe herbs for his complaint.

Several men were too badly lacerated to save. One man had received a thrust which opened his bowels. Friends brought him to me upon a pallet but he died as I began to cleanse the wound.

I learned when the battle was over that Prince Edward had taken two hundred French knights and men-at-arms prisoner. Three hundred of Limoges died in the fight, and forty English. Much booty was taken, to enrich nobility, knights, and common soldiers. Among the dead was John de Boys, who, men said, was cut down when he valiantly attacked three French knights. 'Twas of no use bringing him to me, his friends said. He died where he lay.

Jean de Cros, Bishop of Limoges, who it was had surrendered the city to the Duke of Berry a month earlier, escaped injury. But others died because of his perfidy.

A few wounded men remained to be stitched together as night fell, so I finished the work with light from three cressets. 'Twas full dark as I stumbled along the path to my tent. Several men of Lord Gilbert's cohort, Arthur and Uctred amongst them, celebrated victory before a fire, consuming too much of the wine they had seized in the looting of the city. Had I not been so weary I might have made merry with them. Instead I sought first a bucket of water with which to wipe away the blood I had accumulated in the past hours, and then my bed.

Chapter 13

Sir John must learn that the man who slew his son was dead, so next morn I sought him. His appearance was much improved. The ointment I had prepared for his ear, he said, had much reduced the ache. I told him then of John de Boys' death without naming the man.

"'Twas one of his friends, then, who did the murder, as you suspected," said Sir John. "Else you would not know of the guilty man nor that he was slain yesterday."

When I did not immediately reply he said, "Only two of my men-at-arms died yesterday. Walter Eppingham and John de Boys. Walter and Sir Simon were not close. 'Twas John, then, who did murder. But why?"

I made no reply.

"I can guess," Sir John answered his own question. "I told him evil would follow, did he persist in his perversion. Liked lasses well enough. Why could he not keep to them? But what son," he sighed, "listens to his father? 'Twill cost me a fortune to pay priests to say masses for his soul, else he will remain in purgatory ten thousand years."

Some sons listen to their fathers, I thought. I regarded well my own father's advice. Perhaps it depends upon the father as well as the son as to whether the younger observes the admonitions of the elder. And if a legion of priests may pray Sir Simon from purgatory into heaven, what use then of a hell?

Now that Limoges was returned to Prince Edward's rule I wished to return to England. Some of the prince's knights and men-at-arms must remain in Limoges, of course, to oversee rebuilding the wall and make certain that the Duke of Berry did not return. I prayed that Lord Gilbert's cohort would not be amongst those who must stay.

The prince had come near to bankruptcy a few years past

due to the battle of Najera, which he and Pedro the Cruel had won. Victory can be as costly as defeat.

He had raised taxes in Aquitaine and Limousin to restore his empty purse, thus angering the burghers of Limoges and elsewhere, and providing a foothold for the French king.

Recapturing Limoges had surely cost Edward a considerable sum. He would need to raise taxes again, thus reminding the folk of Aquitaine why they had rebelled against his rule, and giving them cause to do so again. The ransom of two hundred knights and gentlemen would go far in reducing Prince Edward's debts, but a costly English army must remain in Aquitaine. I wished not to be a part of it.

For my part the battle for Limoges was over. I had done all asked of me. I had treated the battle wounds of soldiers, solved a murder, escaped the gallows, and offered physic to a great prince. Having fulfilled my responsibilities and more, I deserved to return to my home.

From Sir John's tent I walked to Lord Gilbert's. I had been much relieved during the battle that I had not seen him in the surgery tent.

"Hah, Master Hugh. You have survived the contest. Did I not tell you that you would be in no peril?"

"You did, but we have not yet crossed the sea back to England."

"Well, we shall do so soon enough. Prince Edward wished me to remain here, but although I have served him without payment to this day, the forty days which I owe him are long past and I told him I cannot continue to bear the cost of my retinue without reimbursement.

"And what of Sir Simon's death?" he continued.

"The man who did the felony died yesterday in taking the city."

"You are sure of this?"

"Aye, quite sure."

"Come. The prince will want to hear of this, and how it is that you are certain of it. He speaks of the mystery frequently."

I followed Lord Gilbert through the camp, which since the capture of the city was filling with carts laden with loot. My service at the surgery meant that I was safe from French axes and pikes, but it also meant that I had no part in taking the city and enriching myself at Limoges's expense. If, when an army approaches, a city immediately surrenders, custom requires that it must not be plundered. Fees and taxes and ransoms may be levied. But if a siege is required to take a city, with the noisome conditions a siege army must endure, then the victors are free to seize what booty they may. I would have liked one of Limoges's famed enamels to present to Kate. But she must be content with only my return, empty-handed as 'twill be.

Many men sought Prince Edward's counsel, so Lord Gilbert and I waited till he had rendered judgment upon sundry other matters.

"Ah, Lord Gilbert... when will you be off?" he said. "Soon, no doubt. Crossing to England will be a disagreeable experience anon."

"Two days, I think. You are well served to hold the city, I think, so my lads are dispensable."

"Aye. When the wall is rebuilt Limoges will be secure against King Charles."

"Unless he can find Cornish miners to employ," Lord Gilbert chuckled.

"And Master Hugh," the prince said, turning his attention to me. "Thomas Arderne praises your work. One of my squires," he added when I responded with a blank look. "You sewed his leg back together yesterday. Some Frenchman smote him from the rear and the thrust caught him behind his cuisse."

"I remember. 'Twas a deep slash."

"Will he walk evenly again, or will the cut render him lame?"

"I cannot say. I told him that he must support his weight with a crutch for a fortnight, perhaps more. He was displeased. 'Folk will think me an invalid,' he said. I told him that such a verdict would be proper. For a fortnight he will be an invalid. And if he dispenses with the crutch too soon, the wound may not knit properly and he will then walk with a limp till men carry him to the churchyard."

"Master Hugh has discovered who murdered Sir Simon Trillowe," Lord Gilbert said.

"Ah, and who is the villain?" Prince Edward asked.

"Was," I said, "not is. The man died yesterday in taking Limoges."

"You are sure of this?"

"Aye. There can be no doubt. When I placed the evidence before him he admitted the felony."

"Oh... knew he would hang for his offense, so chose to die in battle rather than do the sheriff's dance. Is that how it was?"

"Aye, m'lord. As you say."

"Who was the fellow?"

"I promised the man that I would not disclose his name."

Prince Edward lifted his brows at this. "What? Not even to your prince?"

From the corner of my eye I saw Lord Gilbert raise one eyebrow, surely startled at my disrespect.

"Well, I applaud a man who keeps his word, and a promise is a promise. Was it your suggestion," Prince Edward continued, "that the felon seek an honorable death in battle rather than twisting at the end of a hempen rope?"

"I may have mentioned the option."

"Hah. A diplomat as well as a surgeon. I could find use for such as you. My father is aged and I may soon come into my kingdom. I think then I shall steal you from Lord Gilbert and have you serve me in London. A surgeon and a cunning agent in one."

I had then the wish that King Edward III continue a long life. Ten years earlier the thought of serving at court would have delighted me, but now I had no higher ambition than to serve Lord Gilbert in Bampton and live peacefully with my Kate. I hoped that my face did not betray the thought. 'Tis not wise to offend royalty, and by withholding a felon's name I had already done so.

True to his word, Lord Gilbert instructed all of his cohort to ready themselves to depart Limoges on Saturday, the twenty-second day of September. We traveled with nearly eight hundred others also eager to reach England before autumn made the sea into a slate-gray grave for unwary voyagers.

Eight hundred men retracing their path through France found great difficulty in finding provender for men and beasts. We had foraged the route but a month before and found little enough sustenance then. But to break up our force would be unwise. Scouts reported that King Charles's men followed closely, eager to seize any who fell behind. There may be strength in numbers, but there is also hunger. My runcie's ribs showed plainly and my own were nearly as visible when we at last came in sight of Calais and the sea.

The harbor sheltered only a dozen or so ships when we arrived at the port. Rank does have its rewards, and few barons of the realm outrank Lord Gilbert Talbot. Others would have to wait. Lord Gilbert's men, me amongst them, went aboard ships and awaited a favorable wind.

For three days a gale blew from the northwest and held us in port. But on the fourth day the sun appeared and the wind shifted so that it came from the south. Sails were raised at dawn and our fleet stood out from Calais, sails bright in the slanting sun.

I had seen the white cliffs rise from the sea once before, when I returned to England as a youth after one year spent studying surgery in Paris. Upon that occasion I was filled with apprehension for what my future might hold. This time no such anxiety assailed me. The Lord Christ had directed my path through pleasant places. I had Kate, two daughters, and every prospect of sons in the years to come. Galen House was more than I could have dreamed of a decade past, and in my service to Lord Gilbert as surgeon and bailiff I had found satisfaction and modest wealth. I had also gained a few scars.

Even Lord Gilbert found little reason to linger at the abbeys and castles between Dover and Oxford where we found succor at the end of each day of travel. There was no lady to welcome him home at Bampton Castle, but likely he was as eager to see his son as I was to take Bessie and Sybil in my arms.

We spent half a day in London. Lord Gilbert wished to pray and light candles at St. Paul's in thankfulness for the success of our campaign and safety for his cohort. Only three of his men-at-arms had suffered wounds and these were slight.

Three days after leaving London I saw the spire of St. Beornwald's Church above the autumn-browned leaves of Lord Gilbert's forest. We all spurred our beasts so as to hurry the last miles, and within half an hour men and beasts clattered across the drawbridge and flooded into the castle yard. This space was immediately filled with the joy of those returning, and those who had prayed for our safe homecoming.

I was yet mounted, and so searched over the heads of the happy throng for my Kate. I found her at the top of the stairs leading to the solar. She had heard the uproar and left the chamber to learn its cause.

Kate caught sight of me, gathered her cotehardie, and with Bessie trailing, plunged down the stairs. I dismounted and ran to meet her. I had looked forward to her embrace for many weeks. As I held her close I felt a swelling come between us. I looked down and contemplated my wife's belly. 'Twas not so slender as when I departed Bampton.

I held Kate at arm's length and spoke. "We are soon to be five?"

She did not reply, but a tear began to flow down her cheek. I thought 'twas from happiness that I had returned. Not so.

"Nay, husband. We will be four."

I was puzzled. I looked to Bessie, who had fixed herself to my leg, and then Kate's words pierced my heart. Where was Sybil?

"Two days after Lammastide," Kate sobbed, "Sybil took a fever. I gave her damson root and sow thistle which I found in

145

your chest, for I have heard you speak of these herbs as useful to treat fevers."

She fell silent.

"These had no effect?" I asked.

Kate shook her head.

"The fever worsened?"

"Aye. Upon the fourth day she died."

Had I not been with Lord Gilbert in France, might I have saved her? Likely not. I am a surgeon, not a physician, and even physicians will not cure all children who suffer such a malady. But yet, for many months to follow, if I lay awake of a night and sleep eluded me, I considered if I might not have healed my daughter's affliction. And perhaps, had I been with Kate, my presence might have softened the blow of Sybil's death for her. Two may carry a burden better than one.

"She is in the churchyard?" A foolish question.

Kate nodded, too overcome with sorrow mixed with joy to speak.

"I wish to go there."

I lifted Bessie to my arms, took Kate by the hand, and together we walked slowly from the castle and the happy throng there to the bridge over Shill Brook, thence to Church View Street. Past Galen House we did not speak, and when we passed under the lych gate Kate pointed to the west end of the church, west of the porch, where it is that in Bampton deceased infants and children are buried.

"I had a coffin made for her," Kate said as we approached a place where the sod had been recently displaced. "And a willow wand lies within it beside her, to ward off the evil one."

To this moment my eyes had remained dry, but as we stood over Sybil's grave Bessie pressed her cheek close to mine, and I felt there the wetness of the child's tears. The little lass was old enough that her parents' sorrow was made her own. My tears mingled with hers.

I would have preferred to spend the night at Galen House, away from the revelers who celebrated a successful campaign and safe return with too much ale and too much noise. The merrymaking which I could not share did not subside till past midnight, but even then I could not sleep.

So it was that next morn I was haggard and unkempt when Lord Gilbert found me. He had been told of our loss, and commiserated. He understood sorrow, having lost Lady Petronilla to plague.

"You may remain here, in the castle, for as long as you wish," he said. "I've no other use for Lady Petronilla's chamber, and with so many knights yet in my employ and feeding at my table, two more mouths will make no difference to the cook.

"But no, you will want to return to Galen House. I can see it in your eyes. Arthur and some others can assist you, tomorrow or whenever you will."

"This day, I think," I replied. "But I do esteem your good will."

*

'Twas a cold, misty day in mid November, a fortnight after Kate and I had returned to our life at Galen House, when I had business at the castle and heard the report of the death of Sir Charles de Burgh.

"The weather was foul," Lord Gilbert said solemnly, "when Sir Charles reached Calais some days after we left the town. He and many others waited more than a week for a fair wind. When it finally came many ships set sail for Dover, but the wind turned, as can happen so late in the season, and a gale drove five vessels upon the rocks near to Folkestone."

"Sir Charles's was amongst these?" I asked.

"Aye. His corpse washed ashore on the shingle next day."

"Sir Charles told me that Lady Joan is with child," I said.

"Aye. Well, he has already a son to inherit his lands and title. But another would be desirable."

"Just in case."

"Aye," Lord Gilbert agreed. "Your Sybil is proof that much can go amiss with children. One heir is not enough... which is why I must seek a wife. I have but Richard, though he seems hale enough."

"So did Sybil, when we departed for France," I said.

"Ah... you take my point readily."

Limoges was taken, but at great cost to many who served Prince Edward.

The Lord Christ told His followers that they must daily take up their cross and follow Him, but most men prefer to take up a sword. Swords are not so heavy as crosses.

Afterword

Prince Edward did not live to become King Edward IV, dying in June 1376, before his father. His second son, Richard, became king when yet a child. Edward was known in the fourteenth century as Edward of Woodstock, not the "Black Prince". That name was not commonly used for him until the Tudor era, so I have avoided it in this tale. The "Black Prince" sobriquet was supposedly applied to Edward because of his black armor, although there is no contemporary evidence for this. His crest featured an unusual black background, and so may have been the source of the nickname.

Historians differ as to the cause of Edward's lingering and debilitating illness. Amebic dysentery and malaria are usually at the top of the list as suspected maladies. Dysentery seems the most likely culprit.

Jean Froissart, a fourteenth-century writer, claimed that the death toll in the capture of Limoges was three thousand. This slaughter has darkened Edward's memory, but is almost certainly enlarged from reality by a factor of ten. It is unlikely that the total population of Limoges in 1370 was more than two thousand. A contemporary source from the Abbey of Saint-Martial in Limoges records three hundred civilian casualties, killed and wounded, which was about one-sixth of the normal population, and sixty of the garrison. A recently discovered letter from Edward to the Count of Foix mentions two hundred prisoners taken, but no casualties are numbered.

Master Hugh and Kate would have been heartbroken about Sybil's death, but not surprised. About one in five of fourteenth-century infants died before their first birthday, and many more children succumbed to illness before they reached maturity.

Bampton Castle was, in the fourteenth century, one of the largest castles in England in terms of the area contained within the curtain wall. Little remains of the castle but for the gatehouse and a small part of the curtain wall, which form a part of Ham Court, a farmhouse in private hands. The current owners are doing extensive restoration work.

Many readers have asked about medieval remains in the Bampton area. St. Mary's Church is little changed from the fourteenth century, when it was known as the Church of St. Beornwald. The May Bank Holiday is a good time to visit Bampton. The village is a morris dancing center, and on that day holds a day-long morris dancing festival.

Village scenes in the popular television series *Downton Abbey* were filmed on Church View Street, and St. Mary's Church appeared in several episodes.

The Bampton town library building, now four hundred years old, was transformed into the Downton hospital for the television series. The building needs extensive repairs and the village would surely appreciate contributions to help maintain this historic facility.

Schoolcraft, Michigan
April 2016

Deeds of Darkness

An extract from the tenth chronicle of
Hugh de Singleton, surgeon

Chapter 1

Plague has made travel somewhat safer. Many folk have died of the great pestilence in the past twenty-some years, so that those who yet live can find employment where they will and have no need to rob other men upon the roads and risk a hempen noose. Safer, aye, but not always safe. There will ever be those who prefer to live by the sweat of another man's brow. Hubert Shillside, Bampton's haberdasher and coroner, learned too late that this was so.

'Twas Good Friday, the fourth day of April, in the year of our Lord 1371, that I learned of Shillside's unwanted discovery. I attended the Church of St. Beornwald alone that day, to see and honor the host as it was placed in the pyx, and thence into the Easter Sepulcher. My Kate had given birth two weeks earlier to our son, whom we named John, in honor of the scholar John Wycliffe, who had been my master at Balliol College twelve years past. So Kate remained at Galen House, with Bessie and the babe, until the time for her churching, and I kept house, boiled pottage for our dinners, bought bread from the baker and ale from his wife, and waited impatiently for gander month to be past.

I cannot enter the church porch but that my eyes stray to the sod near to the west end of the church, where it is that Kate saw our infant daughter, Sybil, placed in her small grave eight months past, whilst I was away in France, bid to accompany my employer, Lord Gilbert Talbot, at the siege and recapture of Limoges.

Perhaps one day I will enter the church porch and not remember the child. I pray not. She has gone before her mother and me, escaping early from the land of death and exchanging it for the land of eternal life.

Father Simon dismissed the congregation after a linen shroud was placed over the pyx, and the velvet curtain drawn across the opening to the Easter Sepulcher. With other Bampton residents – all of us somber, as the remembrance of the Lord Christ's sacrifice to free men from the penalty of their sins came fresh to mind – I departed the church and stepped from the porch into a cold, misty rain. 'Twas appropriate to the day. Good Friday should not be warm and cloudless. Sunshine should be reserved for Easter Sunday.

Half way from the porch to the lych gate I felt a tug upon my sleeve and heard my name called. 'Twas Will Shillside who accosted me.

"My father has not returned from Oxford," he said. I had not known that he had traveled there.

"He went there on business?" I asked.

"Aye. Departed on Tuesday. Was to return to Bampton last eve. Thought perhaps he'd become weary, carryin' a sackful of goods, an' sought lodging for the night, mayhap at the abbey in Eynsham."

"If he did so," I replied, "he would surely have returned by now."

"Aye. That's why I'm troubled."

Will Shillside was a youth of twenty or so years, his beard in the process of changing from gossamer threads to bristles, and his formerly scrawny body filling out. Last June he had wed Alice atte Bridge, and it was become clear that Hubert Shillside would be a grandfather before this summer was done. Unless some misfortune had befallen him upon the road to or from Oxford.

"What business had he in Oxford?" I asked.

"He travels there for the goods he sells here. I told him that I would go, but he insisted that I am unskilled in business matters and would be gulled by the men of Oxford who supply the stuff we sell."

"Pins and buttons and buckles and such," I said.

"Aye. And ribbons, and spools of linen and silken thread this trip."

"Aye. I did mention to your father some weeks past that my supply of silken thread is near depleted."

Silken thread is of value to me in my service as surgeon to the folk of Bampton and nearby places. I trained for one year in Paris, returned to Oxford, and found employment as both surgeon and bailiff to Lord Gilbert Talbot, lord of the manor of Bampton and its castle. When folk lacerate themselves at their work, or drop stones or beams or axes upon their toes, silken thread is useful to stitch them back together again.

But it was as bailiff that Will Shillside sought me to report his father missing upon the road to Oxford. 'Tis a bailiff's duty to see to the welfare of those of his bailiwick. 'Tis a great misfortune for those of us who do so that many bailiffs do not.

It was too late to set out that day for Oxford. If Shillside had stumbled under his load and fallen into a ditch, it would soon be too dark to see his prostrate form. And if he had toppled and struck his head against a rock and was insensible, he would not hear and respond if we called to him. I told Will that he should come to the castle at dawn. I would gather a few of Lord Gilbert's grooms and instruct the marshalsea to have palfreys ready. Beasts would speed the search, and several pairs of eyes and ears would be better than but two.

Saturday morn dawned clear but cold. I consumed a maslin loaf to break my fast, and a cup of ale, and told my Kate that, depending upon the success or failure of the search, I might return to Galen House yet this day, or on the morrow, or perhaps not. She nodded and kissed me farewell, being well accustomed to a bailiff's tangled schedule.

I wrapped my fur coat about me and set off down Church View Street for Bampton Castle. Will Shillside, his face drawn with worry, was before the gatehouse awaiting me. I was in hope that his father might have arrived home in the night. The dark circles under Will's eyes told me this was not so.

Arthur and Uctred, grooms in Lord Gilbert's service, have proven useful companions when my service as Lord Gilbert's bailiff has required assistance. So I had told them to be ready with beasts saddled as soon as daylight would make a search possible.

Lord Gilbert was not in residence at Bampton Castle. He had spent most of the winter at Goodrich Castle, as was his custom.

155

So life for a groom of Bampton Castle, without the master in residence, was tedious. A search for a missing haberdasher would enliven dull days.

Several ways lead from Bampton to Oxford. Many days would be required to search them all, but Will assured me his father always traveled by way of Eynsham, crossing the river at Swinford. We four did likewise, calling out Shillside's name every hundred paces or so, and keeping eyes upon the verge. There was no response to our shouts, nor any sign of a man who might lie ill or injured near the road.

We passed Osney Abbey and entered Oxford across Bookbinder's Bridge. I asked Will where his father was accustomed to do business in Oxford.

"Martyn Hendy is our usual supplier. Shop is on Fish Street."

We went there. Arthur and Uctred remained with the beasts whilst Will and I sought the proprietor. Hendy is a moon-faced fellow, with an equally circular belly. His business prospers, I think. He remembered Will from past visits, when he had accompanied his father. His greeting brought us no joy.

"Ah, Will... is your father well? He has sent you to do his business rather than attend himself, I see."

"Has my father not called here a few days past?" Will asked.

"Your father? Here, in Oxford? Nay, I've not seen 'im."

Will looked to me with alarm writ across his face. Hendy saw, and spoke.

"Perhaps he has taken his custom elsewhere. Although he'd not get a fairer price than from me."

"The price of such goods is fixed," I said. "Fair or not."

"Aye," the merchant agreed. "So 'tis." He winked at Will.

"Father did not speak of taking his business to another," Will said, ignoring this, "but perhaps he did so."

"Why do you ask this?" Hendy wanted to know.

"Hubert Shillside was to return to Bampton Thursday," I said. "He did not, so I and two others have come with Will seeking him. Where might he have sought supplies if he did not do so here?"

Hendy directed us to three other Oxford merchants who dealt in buttons and buckles and pins and thread and such stuff. We received from these burghers the same answers we had from Hendy. Hubert Shillside had not visited the proprietors. There were no other establishments in Oxford dealing with the kind of goods Shillside wished to purchase. Something had apparently happened to the man while he walked to Oxford four days past. What that might be did not bear thinking about, but bailiffs are employed to consider such things. I must soon earn my wages.

Four men might search for another between Bampton and Oxford for a fortnight and not find him. If Shillside had met with felons who demanded his purse and then slew him, his corpse might be hid in some wood or dumped in the Thames, if he was attacked near to the river. We might never find the man. I did not say this to Will, but I did study the river as we re-crossed Bookbinder's Bridge.

We had passed Osney Abbey when Will said what we all were thinking.

"He's slain, I fear. Some men have seized him and slain him for his purse."

"How much coin did he travel with?" I asked.

"Father usually purchased ten or so shillings' worth of goods. Said to buy less meant to walk to Oxford more often."

"Did he speak to others of his journey? That he would set out for Oxford Tuesday morn?"

"Dunno. Might've, I suppose."

We splashed across the Thames at Swinford and a short time later approached the gates of Eynsham Abbey. Days grew longer. If we pressed our beasts we might reach Bampton by nightfall, but this would be cruel to animals which had already borne us more than twenty miles this day. And I thought the abbot might assist me, if he was told of my search for a missing man and his missing shillings.

Abbot Gerleys owes his place, to some extent, to me. A few years past, whilst I sought the felon who had slain a novice of the abbey, I discovered a heresy among a few of the monks. The

157

leader of this heretical sect was the prior, Philip Thorpe, and but for my learning of his heresy, he would likely have become the next abbot of the house. But Philip was persuaded to transfer to Dunfermline Abbey, in Scotland, where winter lasts till May and each frigid morning will remind him of his sin, and Brother Gerleys became abbot upon the death of the elderly Abbot Thurstan.

The abbey hosteller recognized me, sent for two lay brothers to care for our beasts, and led us to the guest house with a promise that loaves, cheese, and ale would soon arrive. I told the monk that I sought conversation with Abbot Gerleys, and soon after our meal arrived so did the abbot.

This was an honor I did not expect. When a man wishes to speak to an abbot it is he who must, if granted permission, call upon the abbot. Will and Arthur and Uctred were suitably impressed that a man whose presence was required when King Edward called a parliament would deign to seek his humble visitors.

Abbot Gerleys requested more ale be brought, and seated himself across the table from me. When I had last seen the abbot he was a spare, slender, almost emaciated monk. His post evidently suited him, for his cheeks were now rounded and his habit offered a slight bulge where it once had draped flat across his belly.

"How may I assist Lord Gilbert's bailiff?" he said.

I told the abbot of our journey to Oxford and the reason for it. He listened silently, intently, his brow furrowed and lips drawn thin.

"We four," I concluded, "will continue the search for Will's father on Monday, when we return to Bampton. But I have small hope of success. 'Tis a busy season, I know, but if you could assign some lay brothers to leave the abbey and search other roads and byways nearby, I would be much obliged to you."

"It will be done," Abbot Gerleys replied, "and not only for your need. There is much amiss hereabouts. Word has come to me that men have done hamsoken in villages nearby. Two of these are abbey manors. A man was beaten nearly to death in Appleton when he objected to having his oxen taken, and a man from Wytham has gone missing."

"Was he upon the roads, a traveler?" I asked.

"Aye. Not fleeing a harridan wife, so I'm told, but taking sacks of barley to Abingdon a fortnight past. Man, horse, cart, and barley have disappeared."

This was not good to learn. Nothing of the sort had happened near to Bampton, at least not that I had heard – and bailiffs are expected to hear of such things – but if theft and murder are but ten or so miles away, 'tis likely the affliction will spread, as a contagion passes from the ill to the healthy. Why is it, I wonder, that good health does not spread from the vigorous to the sickly, but only the other way round?

I would have preferred to celebrate Easter and the resurrection of the Lord Christ in Bampton, at the Church of St. Beornwald, even if my Kate could not accompany me. Duty and desire are oft in conflict. I and my companions heard Easter Mass at the abbey church, rested our beasts, and after a dinner of roasted capon and loaves with honeyed butter, wandered roads about Eynsham searching for Hubert Shillside. I did not expect to find him in a place where so many folk are about, who would already have discovered a man injured or dead near to a road, and did not. But Will could not remain in the abbey guest house whilst his father might be somewhere near and in distress. So we poked into hedges and climbed over walls and prowled forests with no result but for a sting from the nettles which I found atop a stone wall enclosing an abbey field.

We broke our fast next morning with loaves fresh from the abbey oven and cups of excellent ale. As lay brothers brought our beasts I saw Abbot Gerleys speaking to another band of lay brothers, gesturing to north and south, east and west as he spoke. "Here are the men who will seek your father," I said to Will.

The lad had not slept well. Dark circles under his bloodshot eyes gave him the appearance of a man twice, nay, three times his age.

The abbot concluded his instructions and sent the searchers off, two by two. I thanked him for this aid, bid him send word to Bampton if his lay brothers found any clue to Hubert Shillside's disappearance, then prodded my palfrey through the abbey gate.

Men, women, even children were busy in the fields this day. Some strips had not yet been plowed for spring crops, so teams of oxen and horses were turning the soil. In another field several women worked with dibble sticks, planting peas and beans.

Other fields were being sown to oats or barley or perhaps dredge, and small boys found employment slinging stones and clods at birds who would consume the seed before harrows could cover it with soil.

At several places along the road I stopped and called to laborers, asking them to keep watch for any traveler they might find along the way who had been injured or assaulted. Always these folk agreed to do so, tugging a forelock in appreciation of my status as told them by my fur coat. This garment had been of value two days past, but was now too warm. The spring sun warmed our travel, if not our hearts.

We reached Bampton shortly after noon, having seen no sign of Hubert Shillside nor spoken to any folk who had.

Wednesday, about the sixth hour, two lay brothers rapped upon the door of Galen House. A corpse, they said, was found, stripped of clothing and shoes, in a wood between Eynsham and Farmoor. The body rested now before the altar of the abbey church, and Abbot Gerleys desired that I attend him forthwith to identify the man, for the corpse was putrid and beginning to stink, which interfered with the monks' observance of canonical hours. I felt sure that the dead man was Hubert Shillside, struck down by robbers. Not so.